ON ARCTURUS VII

ON ARCTURUS VII

Eric Brown

NewCon Press
England

First published in the UK August 2021 by
NewCon Press
41 Wheatsheaf Road,
Alconbury Weston,
Cambs, PE28 4LF

NPN011 (limited edition hardback)
NPN012 (paperback)

10 9 8 7 6 5 4 3 2 1

ISBN:

978-1-912950-94-2 (hardback)
978-1-912950-95-9 (paperback)

Cover layout and design by Ian Whates

Typesetting and editorial meddling by Ian Whates
Text layout by Ian Whates

One

I was in my third year of retirement when the business tycoon Santor Vakhodia came to Néos Kyrenia via Telemass with an offer I couldn't refuse – though I didn't welcome his arrival, or the memories his visit provoked.

I'd bought a plot of land on a remote equatorial island, installed a modest habitat dome, and whiled away my days doing very little. I spent my mornings pottering in the garden and my afternoons on the verandah alternately reading and staring out at the great canted rings of the blue-green gas giant of which Néos Kyrenia is the fifth moon. In the evenings after dinner I often walked along the coast and watched the sea as it surged and swilled and dashed itself to scintillating fragments on the crystal spars that form much of the island's coastline.

I had the occasional visitor – old Matthews, a retired professor of geology, dropped by once a week and we played chess and enjoyed a glass or two of local wine. Once a month my daughter flew in from the capital city, a hundred kilometres to the north, and stayed for a couple of days. Perhaps twice a week I strolled into the village in the afternoon and sat outside the taverna, enjoying a glass of ouzo and chatting to the locals. As far as I was concerned, I'd earned my retirement; I had some good memories to look back on, and a few I'd rather have forgotten. I could have had them erased, of course, but I'd read somewhere that the Mem-Erase process could lead to unforeseen cognitive problems.

That afternoon I was pretending to read Homer on my softscreen, while watching the transit of the fourth moon across the pastel face of the gas giant, when my dome's smartcore chimed and a little girl's voice – based on that of my granddaughter, Ella – announced, "You have a visitor at the gate, Jonathan. Shall I allow him entry?"

Matthews never dropped by unannounced in the afternoon, and I did not encourage local callers.

"Who is it?"

"His name is Santor Vakhodia. He has a companion, a Voronian named Stent."

"Patch a visual through to me."

The smartcore projected the image of a middle-aged man standing impatiently before the gate. I made out a hulking, shadowy figure behind him.

"Ask him what he wants."

I stared at the screen hanging in the air before me. My visitor was perhaps forty or fifty, thin-faced, and well-dressed in a grey suit. He was bald, and his skin had a strange glistening pallor which I thought, mistakenly as it turned out, was the result of the Rejuve process.

He frowned as he listened to the smartcore relay my question, then replied – tetchily, judging by his expression.

The smartcore said, "He says he wishes to discuss a 'professional matter' with you."

"What, exactly?"

The smartcore relayed his eventual reply: "He says he can only discuss that with you face to face, but that the outcome of the meeting will be to your advantage."

"Why the Voronian?"

"It is his bodyguard," the smartcore said.

"Very well. Allow him in. But," I went on, "the Voronian remains on a lower level."

The smartcore passed on my proviso. I'd only met a Voronian once before, and its pheromones had left me feeling decidedly sick.

Vakhodia agreed to my demand and the gate swung open. The security camera showed the alien shuffle after its master and halt beside a stand of cacti.

I ordered the smartcore to collapse the screen, and sat up in preparation to receive my visitor.

Vakhodia appeared around the bend of a gravelled pathway and approached the patio. The tight skin of his face stretched in what might have been described as a grudging smile.

His eyes were grey, his lips thin: his was a face that was parsimonious with emotion.

I indicated a seat across the table, and he sat down.

"A drink?" I offered. "Tea, coffee? Or beer?"

"Water, ice cold, will be sufficient," he replied with a precision which suggested that English was not his first language.

I stepped into the dome and drew a pitcher of iced water, and a beer for myself. I carried them out on a tray and placed it on the table.

I poured him a glass of water, watching him. His bird-like gaze flicked about the dome and the garden as if he was assessing their worth and, by extension, my own.

I sat down, picked up my beer and drank.

"How can I help you, Mr Vakhodia?"

He sipped his water, watching me. "I see you have had your implant sealed," he said, indicating the console at my temple.

I sipped my beer. He had not asked a question, after all.

"Might I ask why?" he went on.

I shrugged. "I've retired. I no longer need it."

"And your imp?"

"Disabled," I said.

"Again, might I ask why?"

"I no longer need access to what's happening out there. The business of the Expansion, the political feuds, disasters and whatever. None of it interests me any more. I lead a quiet life," I finished, and cursed myself for sounding defensive.

"You don't miss your work, Mr James?"

"I can't say that I do. I worked for thirty years, saw more of the Expansion than most mortals. And anyway, I knew the way things were going: with the advent of Telemass, starships would be in less and less demand."

I wondered, then, if he wanted me to pilot a ship again. But why? There were hundreds of younger, better pilots than myself out there.

"Why did you stop, Mr James? You were, after all, relatively young at fifty-seven."

He'd done his research, then: but to what end?

"I told you. I saw the way things were going. I got out voluntarily, before economics pushed me out."

He stared at me with his ice-grey eyes, then asked, "What exactly happened on Arcturus Seven?"

I drew a breath, then hid my discomfort with a long drink of beer.

His inquiry suggested he was employed by the Delacroix family, but everything else about him told me that he was not a lawyer, or even an investigator.

"You seem to know a lot about me," I countered. "But I know nothing about you. Who are you, Mr Vakhodia, and what do you want?"

"I am a businessman from Earth, now retired. My line was mining – my family cored the asteroids beyond the Kuiper Belt. Now, in retirement, I pursue my hobbies."

"Which are?"

"I dabble in anthropology, my family history."

"And how do I fit into this?"

He sipped his water, and his gaze slipped past me to regard the vine that shaded my dome.

Surprising me, he said, "Have you read about the starship, *The Pride of Benares?*"

The name was familiar. I dredged my memory, "Wasn't it a slowship that left Earth around two hundred years ago?"

He smiled, or rather his thin lips lifted a little at one end. "It was indeed, Mr James. It journeyed thirty light years, travelling just below c-velocity, and took one hundred and ninety years to reach Gamma Pavonis – ten years ago. By which time, of course, Telemass technology had opened up the stars to humanity. Imagine the reaction of the crew, the colonists, when they awoke from coldsleep to find that all their knowledge had been superseded by advances in science and technology over the two centuries they had been suspended."

"It must have been traumatic, to say the least. But I don't see…"

"*The Pride of Benares* was not the only starship that embarked for the stars at sub-light speeds around two hundred years ago," Vakhodia said. "There were two others, the *Núria Rial,* which has never been discovered and is presumed lost between the stars, and the European Space Agency starship, the *Persephone.*"

I leaned forward. "And this ship?"

"The *Persephone,*" he said, "phased into space-norm at the end of its long journey just two years ago."

I had a stomach-churning presentiment as to where this was leading. "Go on."

"It made landfall on Arcturus Seven," Vakhodia said, "the planet known by its natives as Pharantara."

I shook my head. "How do you know this? Its emergence into space-norm would have made the news. I heard nothing –"

He interrupted, "Because of Pharantara's designation as a Closed Planet, and the delicate nature of the starship's emergence and landfall there, the authorities have understandably enforced a news blackout –"

It was my turn to interrupt. "You said it made landfall?"

9

"The planet is Earth-norm, after all, and within acceptable parameters for colonisation. Of course, the crew of the ship did not know of its Closed Planet designation before landing – just as they were in ignorance of humanity's Expansion."

"How do you know this?"

"I have friends in high places, Mr James."

I sat back, taking this in. I thought of human colonists on Pharantara, and the notion frightened me. Then I considered something else, and said, "But... you said they arrived two years ago. It was hot enough when I... when my team landed there three years ago. It'll be approaching high summer now."

Pharantara, Arcturus VII, describes a highly elliptical orbit about its red giant primary. A full cycle takes it through two relatively short, intensely hot summers each lasting four Terran years, and two long, cold winters – when an ice-age descends and the surface of the world is uninhabitable – each lasting some ten years.

I shook my head. "I pity the poor colonists," I went on. "It's to be hoped they've returned to their coldsleep pods."

I stopped there and stared at him.

I asked, "What do you want from me, Mr Vakhodia?"

"I have hired a smallship to be telemassed to Arcturus Seven," he said, "and I want you as part of my team."

Two

My pulse pounded. I was glad I was seated, or in my surprise I would have made an ungainly attempt to find a seat.

"There are many better pilots than me out there," I protested. "Or you could always equip the smallship with one of those smartnexus AIs that were in development when I retired."

Vakhodia smiled to himself. "The ship I have hired *is* fitted with an AI pilot," he said.

"Then, Mr Vakhodia, what the hell do you want with me?"

He gestured with his right hand; its flesh, like the skin of his face, was so pale it was almost translucent. "You know the world," he said. "Also, you know the natives, the Pharan. I understand that you became, in your short time on the planet, quite close to them."

I wondered how he knew this. "What makes you say that?" I asked.

"I have my sources," was all he would say.

I sat back in my chair and said with a trace of impatience, "Just what do you want on Arcturus Seven, Mr Vakhodia?"

"I have recently become interested in the age when the *Persephone* left from Lunar orbit, bound for the stars. I have been studying the history of my family. My great-great-great grandfather, Santor Vakhodia – after whom I was named – was the man who created the Vakhodian business dynasty. He set up the asteroid mining company that still carries his name. And then, just thirty and bored with everything in the solar system – I rather think he found it claustrophobic – he bought himself a coldsleep berth aboard the *Persephone*." He shrugged, smiling across at me.

"I simply want to meet him," he went on, "and to thank him, face to face."

I sipped my beer, buying myself some time. At last I said, "Why have you been allowed access to the planet before any official contact team?"

He nodded, as if he considered the question entirely reasonable. "The authorities have hired me to act as reconnaissance. I will locate the colonists and report the situation back to the United Space Organisation in due course."

"And you wish to employ me as a guide?"

"You know the terrain, the dangers, and the natives. You would be paid, and paid well, for your services."

"And if I say no?"

"Then I will find someone else to fulfil the role."

I shifted in my seat, uncomfortable at the thought.

"You mentioned the dangers," I said. "They're not inconsiderable. Quite apart from the climate, the searing temperatures, the solar flares and storms, there are the various inimical lifeforms to consider. It was bad enough when we explored the world, three years ago. The creatures that had lain dormant during the ice-age winter were barely stirring – and we had a hard enough time of it then. Now, with high summer even closer…" I smiled at him. "I dread to think of the horrors lurking on the planet."

"We would be well armed, and protected with all that the latest tech can provide."

I stared at this explorer *manqué*, with his fantasies of tracking down a long-lost relative on an exotic world and shaking his hand in thanks.

"I think you underestimate the dangers, Mr Vakhodia," I said. "The lifeforms of Pharantara are unlike anything you might have encountered before. Think of armoured crabs the size of aircars, not only homicidal but ravenous after a decade of dormancy. Then there are the spiders, horrors that erupt from cocoons buried in the jungle's fertile soil: they're practically undetectable and are as lethal as landmines."

"I have read your report," he said. "I know the dangers."

I stared at him. "You don't know the full story what happened there," I snapped.

"Will you tell me?"

"I won't —"

"You lost a member of your crew in circumstances that the USO will not disclose, for reasons only they, and you, understand. Solange Delacroix was your second in command — and also," he went on, staring across at me, "your lover."

I was tempted to throw him out there and then, but curiosity overcame my rage.

"Who told you that?"

Our relationship had never been common knowledge, or the USO might have ensured that we did not accompany each other on exploratory missions. Only the three other members of my crew had known about me and Solange. Evidently one of them had spoken to Vakhodia out of turn, breaking the promise they had made to me at the mission's end.

"That need not concern us here, Mr James," he said smoothly.

I bit back the desire to press him; his continued refusal would only further annoy me.

Instead I said, "I have no desire to return to Arcturus Seven."

He smiled with what I perceived to be self-satisfaction. "You haven't yet heard my offer."

"I can't be bought."

"I do not wish to buy you, Mr James; merely hire your services."

"I have no wish to be at your beck and call on that infernal world."

He sipped his water, set the glass down precisely, then said, "Your daughter is attempting to set up a jewellery design company in the capital here — you have helped her with loans, to the best of your ability, but despite the USO pay-off, you are not a rich man. On Earth, your three grandchildren are beginning university courses that are straining the resources of their parents." He hesitated, then went on, "And your son, Edward, is in mounting debt due to his ongoing treatments to alleviate a life-threatening illness."

He smiled, and I kept my expression rigid and silently cursed him.

"I have the wherewithal to entirely fund your daughter's entrepreneurial ambitions," Vakhodia went on. "I can pay for your grandchildren's education. And I can subsidise Edward's medical care for the rest of his life. All you have to do," he said, slipping a thin hand into the pocket of his suit and withdrawing a rolled up softscreen, is append your palm-print to this pre-prepared contract."

He lay the softscreen on the tabletop and, with one long finger, pushed it across to me.

I sat in silence, raging inside, going over and over the reasons why I shouldn't do his bidding – and the many reasons why I should.

"Go on," he purred, "read it. There are, I assure you, no hidden clauses or pitfalls. It is all very simple, and much to your benefit."

I swallowed and, hating myself for doing so, read the three page contract.

It was, as he stated, simple. I was to be hired as a guide and liaison officer for a period lasting no longer than two months, Terran, starting tomorrow. I would lead a team on the surface of the planet where we would remain until we located the *Persephone* and the colonists. A rider to the contract was that, over and above the monies paid to my various family members, I would receive a million Néos Kyrenian drachma, paid into my personal account, upon my lawyer ratifying the legality of the document.

"It is, I think you'll agree, a tempting offer, is it not?"

I sat back and finished my beer, staring past Vakhodia to the rings of the gas giant as I considered my response.

If I didn't agree to his demands, then he would simply hire someone else to act as his guide – and under no circumstances could I allow that to happen.

"If I were to agree," I said, "there is one stipulation I must make."

"Name it."

"We will be accompanied by the woman who was part of my team on the original mission – Octavia Carrera, currently resident on New Brasilia. A medic and pilot. She too will be paid a million Néos Kyrenian drachma."

"Might I ask the reason you desire her presence, Mr James?"

I could have said: *Because I trust her, and I don't trust you. She is loyal, and will watch my back.*

Instead I said, "We work well as a team, and I value her knowledge and expertise in planetary exploration."

"And if she refuses to accompany us?"

"I have every confidence that she will agree to come along," I said, but didn't tell him why I was so confident. It was gratifying to know that Mr Vakhodia's investigation of my family and friends had not uncovered Octavia's secret.

"I will have my lawyer contact Ms Carrera at once," he said. "And I will be in touch when the amended contract has been drawn up. It has been pleasant making your acquaintance, Mr James."

He rose from the table, inclined his head in farewell, and made his way back down the winding path to the exit.

Minutes later he was joined by the Voronian and I watched his silver aircar rise silently and head inland towards the capital.

That evening, as Deneb set in a blaze of molten glory over the western mountains and the gas giant dipped into the sea to the east, I left the dome and walked along the coastal path. I wanted a drink, but I needed to think through the course of events I had set in motion, my mood tempered by the balm of physical activity.

I thought I had left behind the horrors of Arcturus VII – the remove of light years ameliorating the pain of the memory. In the early days of my retirement, not an hour had passed without images and recollections – along with searing emotions – rearing up from the stew of my unsettled unconscious to plague my waking hours. Over the months and years, time and distance had worked to ease the horror.

Now, against all logic, I had agreed to return to Arcturus VII at the behest of a rich, privileged business tycoon intent on making contact with his great-great-great grandfather.

I had to admit that a return to Pharantara might perhaps work to ease my guilty conscience and, despite the manifest dangers, bring closure to a series of events that still had the power to drag me screaming from nightmare-troubled sleep.

I stared out across the surging waves as the magenta light of sunset grew ever dimmer. Then I hurried home, poured myself an ouzo, and sat on the patio long into the star-filled early hours.

In the dazzling light of morning I was awoken by the chime of the dome's smartcore, and Emma's childish voice telling me that I had an urgent communication from off-world.

I hurried to the lounge, told the smartcore to play the message, and slumped on the settee as Octavia Carrera's image hung in the air before me.

She smiled out at me from the sun-drenched verandah of her beachside villa on New Brasilia. She wore a bright primrose blouse which contrasted with the absolute ebony of her skin.

I instructed the message to start playing.

"Just had the strangest communication from the lawyer of a guy calling himself Santor Vakhodia, Jon. Seems a mission to Pharantara is on the cards, and I'll be half a million dollars richer. This guy said you wanted me along." She frowned. "Thing is, Jon, is this legit? You really want to go back there?" She leaned towards the screen and her smile increased. "Anyway, that's why I'm coming to see you. I'm taking the Telemass relay from here to Néos Kyrenia is three hours, then I'll hire an aircar. I should be at your place in about five hours, okay?" She frowned. "We need to talk. There are things about this guy, Vakhodia… Anyway, see you soon." She waved fingers. "Bye!"

Three

Towards midday I heard the muffled roar of an aircar's turbo approaching the peninsula. I left my dome and wandered through the garden, down the levels, to the gate. The black teardrop of the car was settling beyond the fence when I opened the gate and leaned against the post, watching Octavia climb out.

She's a tall woman — six foot six — and statuesque. She was on my team for five years before I retired. You get close to someone, working in such proximity for so long. I knew her as if she were my sister.

"Well, look at you!" she called out, stretching.

I walked towards her with open arms. We embraced, kissed cheeks.

"Look at me?" I queried.

"Quite the beach bum. What's with the long hair and beard, and is that a paunch I see?"

I took her hand and walked her back up the path. "You look well," I said.

"I'm always well. It's you I worry about. How're things, Jon?"

I nodded. "I'm doing fine. Things are okay, really. I've prepared lunch, but how about a drink, first? Beer?"

"Beer's great," she said, and I moved into the dome while she seated herself at the table.

On my way back out, I paused to look at Octavia through the open door. She wore black knee-length trews, a scarlet bolero and a tricorne, and sprawled in the chair with her long legs crossed at the ankles.

I felt a sudden, overwhelming surge of affection for the woman. We'd been through a lot on Arcturus VII, and shared a secret. I trusted Octavia Carrera as I trusted no one else.

"So how's life on New Brasilia?"

"Free and easy, Jon. It's paradise – it really is. And piloting tugs between the moons is a cinch."

"You don't miss exploration work with the Line?"

"From time to time, yes, I suppose I do. Then I think what I've got at home, and I'm glad I quit the Line."

"How's Garcia?"

She shrugged. "Still the same old feckless Latino as ever." She seemed reluctant to talk about her lover of ten years.

We sat and drank in silence for a minute or two, then I said, "About Vakhodia…"

She held up a hand, its pale palm cross-hatched with dark lines. "First, I want to come clean."

I stared at her. "Meaning?"

She reached into the tiny pocket of her bolero jacket and pulled out a small silver box. She placed it on the table and lifted the hinged lid. We leaned forward and stared at the tiny pile of glistening blue powder within.

"Matha," I said. "I thought you might have run out of it months ago."

"This is the last of it, Jon. The stuff of life," she said. "Literally."

There is little doubt that the alien drug helped to save her life on Arcturus VII, following the attack of the arachnid a week into the mission. She was on the cusp of death for three days, modern medicine having done all it could to sustain her. Then a deputation of the tiny, humanoid aliens came to our camp and – unbeknownst to me – administered a small dose of a drug they called matha to Octavia. It saved her life. In hours, her condition improved, the drug counteracting the poison injected by the arachnid-analogue.

The only downside was that it left her with an addiction to the stuff, though Octavia had not complained. She'd been addicted to far more dangerous drugs in her time. Matha, she said, made her see the world anew, and gave her a mellow high, with minimal withdrawal symptoms.

"It's running low," I said.

"Three months ago I stopped for a month, to see what it would be like." She shrugged. "I sweated some, and my bones ached, but I pulled through A-okay."

"You said you want to come clean," I said.

She stared down at the glittering powder in silence, nodding to herself. She snapped the lid shut, then looked up at me.

"I want to tell you something, Jon. I hope you don't think any less of me when I'm through."

"Go on."

"After what happened to Solange," she said, "when you were suffering... That little alien guy, Tan'lo – you remember him? Well, he said I should give you a dose of the matha they'd given me. He said it would make you feel better, ease your loss, or at least make the pain bearable." She hesitated, not looking at me. "You were in a bad way, Jon. I feared for you. I even thought you might... that Solange's death had sent you over the edge, and you might not want to go on. Thing is" – she looked directly at me now – "I can't work out if I didn't give you any of the stuff because I genuinely feared you'd become hooked – and I knew how you feared addiction of any kind – or because I didn't want to share it, and wanted to keep all of it for myself."

She closed her eyes.

A silence came between us.

I reached out and squeezed her hand, then lifted her fingers and kissed them.

"You did right," I said, "for whatever reason. I didn't need the matha, and I pulled through okay, didn't I?"

She let out a sigh. "It's been on my conscience for years, Jon. Couldn't work out if I was a selfish bitch, or... or whatever. And I still don't know."

"You're honest," I said, "and I value that more than anything. Now, how about lunch?" I went on. "And we can discuss Mr Vakhodia."

We ate tiropeta and salad on the patio, washed down with sharp retsina.

"He came yesterday, unannounced," I said. "And made the offer. A million Néos Kyrenian drachma if I agreed to accompany him to Pharantara as a guide, plus financial assistance to all my family." I told her what he'd said about the *Persephone* and his long-lost ancestor.

"And you reckon he's on the level?"

I shrugged. "I really had no way of telling."

"You didn't trawl the Cloud?"

"I had my imp removed three years ago," I said. "Remember?"

"So you agreed to Vakhodia's offer?"

"Not in so many words. I said that *if* I were to agree, then you must come too. But..." I hesitated. "I would have agreed even if he'd said he didn't want you along." I told her what he'd said about hiring someone else instead of me.

She nodded, her lips pursed around a mouthful of retsina. "Now this is the thing, Jon. After his lawyer contacted me, dangling the cash, I did a bit of research, had my imp hit the Cloud."

"And."

"Nada. According to the Cloud, Mr Santor Vakhodia doesn't exist."

"He's a millionaire," I said, "heir to the Vakhodia mining dynasty. In other words, he's rich enough to have his data trail scrubbed. You know what the rich are like."

She shrugged, dubious. "It's odd that there's nothing at all, though."

21

"But what about his ancestors, and the Vakhodia mining company?"

"Oh, that exists, okay. It's one of the biggest players in the mining racket, spread over a dozen star systems. And the Vakhodia family was influential in Europe a couple of hundred years ago."

"So you're suspicious about Vakhodia and his motives?"

She let the question hang in the air, then said, "I'm not sure. Not sure at all." She shrugged. "Isn't it strange that the USO have asked this businessman to do the groundwork on the *Persephone*? I thought they'd be eager to get in there themselves."

"They're stretched. If he knows people high-up in the USO, twisted a few hands, greased a few palms. He's certainly privy to the confidential reports we made after the mission, so my guess is he does know a few high-ups in the organisation."

"And he wants you as a guide?"

"It's a dangerous place. We've been there, survived. We know the pitfalls."

"You buy that?" she asked.

"Could he have an ulterior motive for going there?"

"The planet has protected status," she said, "because of the natives. What if he had his suspicions about the true nature of the Pharan?"

I smiled uneasily. "How on earth could he?"

"Earlier, you said he seemed to know things that weren't in the report: he knew you'd become 'close' to the Pharan. What if Connor or Lascelles got to know what we discovered – and told Vakhodia?"

I shook my head, vehement. "Connor and Lascelles couldn't know. They were nowhere near when you were attacked and Tan'lo saved you, and what happened after that – and later. There's no way they could possibly know."

"But say they *did* know, somehow, and word got back to Vakhodia – that might be the reason for his interest in the planet. Can you imagine if the USO got wind of what we know? Their protected status would be torn up and they'd put the little guys under the scalpel without a qualm."

"So you're saying that what Vakhodia told me about the *Persephone* and the colonists is a lie?"

She shook her head. "Not a lie, no. I did some digging on that, too. A colony ship called the *Persephone* did leave Lunar orbit a little under two hundred years ago."

"So there you are," I said.

"But what if he's using the *Persephone* and his ancestor as no more than a cover? Perhaps his real motive is to discover the truth about the Pharan."

I thought about it for a while, staring down at my empty glass. "Okay, Octavia. Look at it this way. If I refuse his offer, if we don't go along with him... He's not going to abandon the mission, is he? He said he'd just find someone else to act as his guide. So he'll get whatever he wants in the long run, anyway."

She grunted.

"So if we agree to accompany him, we can keep an eye on him, ensure he doesn't get up to anything. And if he tries something, between us we can stop him."

She stared at me for a long time, then broke into a smile. "That's you all over, Jonathan James. Ultra-logical and proactive. I guess that's why you were the best pilot the Line ever had."

"So am I right, or am I right?" I asked, refilling our glasses.

She took a drink, reflective. "You up to it, Jon?" she asked in a quiet voice. "You sure you can handle going back there?"

"I've thought about that a lot since yesterday. I want to go. Hell, now that it's been offered to me, I can't *not* go. Look, Octavia... I've always believed in facing down your demons, you know that. When Elspeth died, almost twenty years ago... She wouldn't have wanted me to stop sky-diving because of what happened to her, and though it hurt like hell to jump again, I had to do it. For myself. To get over the fear and face my demons." I shrugged. "The same is true now. I want to go. And I want you to come with me." I hesitated, looking across at her. "So what do you say?"

She sipped her drink, her gaze far away as she considered.

"Vakhodia's lawyer gave me a contact number we were to call if we agreed to his request," she said. "Then we were to Telemass to Hennessy's World, where we'll board the smallship." She reached out and tapped the silver box with a long fingernail. "So I reckon we've got ourselves a mission, Mr James – but one thing."

"Name it."

She pointed at the sealed console on the side of my head. "You get your imp uploaded and installed, okay? You'll be needing it."

Four

Octavia and I took a Telemass shot to the junction planet of Amalia, Mu Aure III, and from there made the jump to Hennessy's World. The journey had taken just six hours, and we had an hour to kill before we were due to rendezvous with Vakhodia and his team.

Octavia led me to the revolving cafe set on a cantilever projecting from the Telemass Station's scimitar tripod. While she fetched two coffees from the bar, I sat at a window table and admired the slowly rotating view.

Hennessy's World was largely agricultural, and the Telemass Station was set amid miles of rolling farmland, a variegated patchwork of a dozen different crops. Two moons rode high in the blue sky, a ivory giant and its smaller red companion.

Beside the Station was an extensive spaceport where more than fifty smallships squatted in their berths. I wondered which one might be ours. I had not been aboard a 'ship for three years, when I had piloted my own vessel away from Arcturus VII. Now I would be a mere passenger, returning to that world.

It was an odd sensation to be connected to my imp again, at once novel and yet familiar. For all my working life, some thirty years, I'd had its presence riding in my head – a source of almost limitless knowledge at my instant command.

On my retirement, I'd elected to have my imp wiped, along with the running programs that had allowed me to pilot smallships for the Taurus Line. I could have kept the imp, but something – perhaps subconsciously I wanted to deny myself its luxury as some form of punishment – made me decide otherwise.

For months afterwards the silence in my head often became hard to tolerate. I wanted its voice there, or the music it would play at my command, to drown out my thoughts about the events on Arcturus VII. But I did not relent: I chose to live with the guilt. Perhaps only through suffering, I told myself, would I find peace.

"Imp," I thought, "do you still have the audio cache from 1st December '71?"

I do.

I steeled myself. I wanted to hear Solange's voice, one last time. "Then play it," I thought.

I closed my eyes and listened.

I was transported. I was on Lysenko again, taking a break between shifts. We had made love in the A-frame on the beach and were holding each other, and Solange was whispering in my ear: "*My life changed when we met, Jonathan. I was unhappy, and you cured me. You made me whole.*"

I'd kept the cache and had my imp replay it when our shifts meant that Solange and I were apart. It was heartening to be reminded that I'd made a difference to the life of someone as special as Solange Delacroix.

Now I had meant to listen to it for one last time, then order my imp to wipe it for good. But something would not let me issue the command.

"Jon," Octavia said. "You all right?"

I opened my eyes and smiled. "I'm fine."

"Talk about a mask of tragedy. What the hell were you thinking about?" She placed a coffee before me and sat down. "Don't tell me – Solange, right?"

"Touché."

She took my hand. "It's going to be tough, but you'll be fine. And I'll be with you all the way, okay?"

I squeezed her hand in thanks.

A loudspeaker relayed the information that the next beam was due in three minutes, directly from Paris, Earth.

I glanced at the time on my wrist-com. "That'll be Vakhodia and his team."

The café ceased turning, its viewscreen aligned now with the station's reception pad to give the diners a grandstand view of the tachyon vector's arrival.

Around us, people pressed up against the plexiglass and murmured in anticipation. We joined them, and I stared down at the hexagonal deck, marked with abstruse mathematical decals and calibrations. Engineers made final preparations, then retreated behind steel baffles as the countdown began.

"Ten... Nine... Eight..."

I peered down at the reception pad with the rest of the observers, as excited as they were at the prospect of the imminent, miraculous arrival of the travellers. After all, it wasn't every day that I witnessed human beings reconstituted after their bodies had been stripped down and fired fifty light years through space.

"Three... Two... One..."

Octavia leaned forward, her eyes wide.

A blinding bar of golden light hit the reception pad in eerie silence. I blinked, and in that fraction of a second the golden light vanished and was replaced by fifty men and women, frozen in the postures they had adopted light years away on Earth. Then the tableau broke up as they strode across the deck to the reception lounge and immigration control.

I made out Santor Vakhodia accompanied by the rhino-like bulk of his Voronian bodyguard, Stent, who shuffled alongside him. To the tycoon's right was a short, compact man in a deactivated camouflage suit: he looked like a hired thug.

Due to the pheromones exuded by the Voronian, their fellow travellers were giving them plenty of room.

"Strange," I said as the trio passed into the reception lounge. "When he said 'team', I thought he meant an entire retinue of servants and hangers on. Perhaps the others arrived earlier?"

"Or Vakhodia likes to run a tight ship," Octavia said.

We left the cafe and took the escalator to the arrival's lounge and waited for Vakhodia and his companions to be processed.

"Ever met a Voronian?" I asked as we waited.

She pulled an expressive face. "Once. And I vomited."

"Try not to throw up this time, okay?"

"Afraid we'll make a bad impression in front of the tycoon and his lackeys?"

I smiled. "We have the image of intrepid explorers to uphold."

Octavia merely laughed at me.

"Here they are," I said.

As the sliding door opened, Vakhodia and his henchmen were the first to stride through, and I wondered if he'd paid his way to the head of the queue.

He saw me and raised a hand in greeting, then said something to the Voronian who trundled away from us and waited by the exit.

"Mr James," Vakhodia said, and even managed a smile, "and Ms Carrera: delighted to make your acquaintance."

The man in the camouflage suit hung back, giving me the once-over. The millionaire turned to him and made the introductions. "This is Šarović," Vakhodia said, "and my Voronian, Stent," he went on, nodding across to the alien. "I have two cars waiting to take us to the port, if you'd care to follow me."

We left the Telemass Station, and the four of us boarded a limousine for the short journey. To spare us, the Voronian travelled in his own vehicle.

We passed through the spaceport security control and crossed the tarmac to the waiting smallship. I was impressed: no expense had been spared. The ship was a Titan class Interceptor with a twin neutron drive: a bulky jet-black triangle sitting on ramrod stanchions like some eerily alien insect. The 'small' in smallship was far from descriptive: the ship was huge – a hundred metres from nose to tail, and half as tall.

Vakhodia ushered us up a ramp and into a plush lounge. Šarović made himself scarce, and the Voronian was nowhere in sight. I wondered if the alien would be travelling in the hold.

"If you would excuse me while I oversee the jump to the station," Vakhodia said, and stepped from the lounge.

Minutes later the ship's engine ignited, sending a muffled roar through the craft. The smallship lifted slowly, turned on its axis, and made a parabolic jump to the Telemass Station.

Šarović appeared at the doorway. "Mr Vakhodia requests your presence on the bridge," he said.

We followed him through the door, along a short passage, and emerged onto the amphitheatre of the bridge. The familiar architecture of the smallship's control room brought back a slew of memories, though I was disconcerted to see that the pilot and co-pilot's slings had been removed – unnecessary accoutrements now that the ship was controlled by an AI.

Vakhodia stood at the far end of the chamber before the delta viewscreen. We descended and joined him. Šarović followed, taking up a position to the tycoon's right.

I looked through the viewscreen as the towering form of the Telemass Station loomed closer, a collection of domes and cantilevered observation posts sitting atop three scimitar legs, with the reception pad centre stage. We slowed, hovered, and came down gently on the deck.

As we stared out, the countdown commenced. Beside me, Octavia stood with her arms folded across her chest. I gripped the handrail and prepared myself for the transition.

"Three... Two... One..."

A golden light enveloped us. I felt a nanosecond's disorientation – a slight warmth zap through my head – and I blinked. In that instant we were beamed hundreds of light years through space.

Beyond the viewscreen I gazed at the velvet immensity of deep space, glittering with a scatter of stars. The closest, the red giant of Arcturus, burned steadily before us. It was a sight I thought I'd never see again.

"It never ceases to amaze me," Vakhodia murmured to himself – and I thought that it was the first statement I had heard pass his lips that hinted at the man's humanity.

"We are due to make landfall in ten hours," he went on. "I suggest we all get some rest."

He strode from the bridge, leaving us in the company of his right-hand man. Šarović leaned against the hand-rail, picking at his teeth with a fingernail.

Octavia eyed him. "Old hand at this game, right?"

He flicked her a glance. "Could say I'm a vet."

"Military, right?"

"Twenty years with the Extrasolar Territorials," he bragged.

His camouflage suit, I saw now at closer quarters, was sophisticated combat wear made up of graphite spars and zirconium inlays.

"So you served in the Antares conflict?" Octavia said.

"Led the platoon that established a bridgehead on the crabs' homeworld. We wiped the bastards out, payback for what they did to the Edenwold colony. The Antareans might've known how to slaughter innocent colonists, but they were no match for the Territorials."

"I understand you were sent in to quell the unrest on Garibaldi," she said, glancing at me.

He shrugged. "We were following orders. How the hell did we know the generals got it wrong?"

"I heard a thousand civilians bought it in a neutron strike?"

"Exaggeration," he snapped. "I reckon it was less than a hundred."

As if, I thought, that made it any less of a war crime.

"You served after that?" I asked.

"Here and there," he hedged.

Octavia changed tack. "How did you get involved with Vakhodia?"

"I was freelancing after I served my time. Mr Vakhodia wanted someone he could rely on for protection, in every situation. He hired the best."

"You and the Voronian?"

"The alien keeps unwanted people away," he said. "I deal with those who might get through. So far," he went on, grinning from Octavia to me, "no one has."

Octavia nodded, as if impressed. "So what gives on Pharantara, Šarović? Just what does Vakhodia want there?"

"He must've told you – he's tracking down his ancestor and reporting back to the USO."

"How long have you worked for him?" she asked.

"A little over six months, Terran."

"And you trust him?"

The mercenary gave that annoying grin again. "I trust anyone who pays me a thousand crowns a week."

I said, nodding at his suit, "That's some get-up."

He grinned. "The best." He moved from the rail and stood before me. "Ever seen one of these in action?"

"Can't say I have."

"Like a demonstration?" He was like a kid with a new toy.

"Go ahead," I said.

He moved to the centre of the chamber, where the slings would have hung before the refit. He turned and stared across at us, hands on hips. He must have given a sub-vocalised command because, as we watched, the collar of his suit shifted, moved, flowed up and around his face and head – a contour-hugging silver mesh of zirconium circuitry.

Then he disappeared.

One second I was staring at the squat mercenary – then he'd vanished.

I exchanged a glance with Octavia.

I stared at where Šarović had stood, then looked left and right, searching for the telltale flicker where the suit's circuitry lagged behind his movement. I made out nothing.

Then, surprising me, his voice called out from across the bridge, ten metres from where he'd vanished. "Pretty impressive, yeah?"

I repressed a smile. "It is," I said, humouring him.

I caught a brief shimmer in the air a couple of metres to our right. He was approaching us, and I braced myself for some kind of assault.

Making me jump, Octavia turned and lashed out, lightning fast. I heard her fist connect with the invisibility suit, followed by Šarović's startled exclamation. The suit's panels flickered as they attempted to compensate for his sudden sprawling movement.

Octavia said, "Don't you ever, ever, do that again, you little bastard. Because, suit or no suit, I'll rip off your balls and choke you with 'em. Got that?"

If I expected the mercenary to show himself and apologise for what he'd done, I'd misjudged his character. I saw a frantic flicker of polychromatic light as he picked himself up and rushed away from us. The suit adjusted to his flight, and the next thing I knew, the door to the bridge slid open and he made his ignominious, if invisible, exit.

"Arsehole!" Octavia said.

"One-nil to you," I said. "I think you've made an enemy there, Octavia."

"I swear, if the little runt touches me again..."

We left the bridge and made our way to the crew quarters, where I found a berth and prepared myself to sleep while the AI carried us towards Arcturus VII.

Five

I came to my senses groggily, disoriented for a moment before recalling where I was.

I looked up. Octavia stood in the doorway, smiling at me.

"We've landed," I said. "How long have you been awake?"

"Just a few minutes."

I washed my face with wipes from the dispenser, then joined her. "Lead the way."

I followed Octavia along the corridor to the bridge, then halted outside the sliding door.

"Jon?" she said, concern in her voice.

"We'll see it, through the viewscreen," I said. "Pharantara. I never thought…"

She reached out and touched my arm. "You'll be fine, Jon. Okay?"

"I'll be fine," I said, more to reassure myself than Octavia.

I stepped forward. The door slid open with an electronic wheeze and I walked through onto the bridge.

The first thing that struck me was the riot of movement and colour beyond the viewscreen.

My previous experience of Pharantara had been three years earlier, when the planet had been a little further way from its primary, and that had been hellish enough. The temperature during the day had been an average of 110 degrees Fahrenheit, and in the dead of night it never dropped below ninety. We had made the smallship our base and conducted our explorations from its safety, venturing out at dawn and dusk.

Now I looked out at a phantasmagorical, writhing chaos of snaking vines, erupting trees, great trumpet blooms that rose as we watched, opened and withered in minutes. We had landed in a gap between trees thirty metres tall, and on its approach the smallship had burned an area a hundred metres in diameter. Even as we looked on, vegetation burst through the blackened undergrowth and reasserted itself, thrashed and writhed in a constant, irrevocable surge to gain dominion and reach for the succour of the sunlight. I saw no wildlife out there, but knew that the fauna of this world would be unlikely to leave the shade: it would be skulking in the shadows, ever watchful, biding its time before it pounced on unwary prey and feasted.

Vakhodia and Šarović noted our arrival with a brief glance, then turned back to stare in wonderment at the circus of rampant life beyond the viewscreen.

I said in a whisper, "It's hell out there."

"One hundred and thirty in the shade," Vakhodia informed us.

I looked up, past the serrated leaves of the jungle canopy high above the smallship, and stared at the sun as it sent out slow motion loops and geysers of molten ejecta in a display that was both majestic and terrible. I broke out into a sweat just staring at the fiery orb.

I noticed that Šarović had slunk away and was standing on the far side of Vakhodia, studiously ignoring Octavia as he gave his full attention to the scene outside.

"Where's the *Persephone*?" Octavia asked.

I looked at Vakhodia. It was some while before he replied. "Ah... I had hoped to come down as close to the ship as possible —"

"And?" I asked, fearing the worst.

"The AI located the starship from orbit, then descended and took us over the area where it came down. It scanned for a suitable landing place close by, but the terrain was mountainous. It would have been suicidal to attempt a landing."

"So," Octavia said with barely concealed impatience, "just how far away are we?"

"A little over one hundred kilometres," he said.

I stared at him. "One hundred!" I laughed. I could not help myself. The idea of attempting to penetrate such hostile jungle – a kilometre of it, never mind a hundred – was preposterous. "How the hell...?"

He said, "We have come prepared for all eventualities, Mr James. There is a crawler in the hold–"

"Even so..." I said, hardly mollified. "One hundred kay in a crawler, no matter how well equipped, through jungle and rocky terrain? Are you sure you couldn't get us closer?"

Vakhodia turned and stared at me. "The AI was adamant on that point," he said with ice in his voice. "As a semi-sentient entity, it is programmed with a prime directive: to ensure the safety of its human charges. Even if I commanded it to attempt a closer landing, it would refuse."

I matched his stare. "Then deactivate the AI," I said, "and I'll take us closer." I looked across at Octavia, and she backed me up with a nod.

Vakhodia gave me one of his malice-tipped smiles as he replied, "When it comes to placing my trust in either an AI pilot, Mr James, or a human being – no matter how qualified – I will choose the AI *every* time."

He allowed a second or two to elapse, then went on, "We will proceed aboard the crawler, Mr James, embarking in approximately two hours."

"Just a moment," Octavia said. "The *Persephone*. You said we overflew the ship. Did you get aerial footage? Is there any sign of life?"

Vakhodia gave a command, and the scene outside the viewscreen disappeared, overlaid with a view of the planet from low orbit. The scene expanded, zoomed in to show a range of rumpled mountains, bare rock for the most part with slashes of green in the valleys between the peaks.

Octavia pointed, and I made out the broken-backed shape of the starship. It had come down heavily, that much was obvious, crash-landing in a narrow jungle-filled valley.

"Any sign of survivors?" she asked.

Vakhodia hesitated, then said, "From these shots, we are unable to tell."

He ordered further magnification, and the view blurred and resolved itself. We stared at a great vertical rent in the side of the starship, through which the jungle had worked its way. There was no sign of human activity down there, or any suggestion that there had been at any point during the past two years.

Vakhodia said, "Perhaps we'll find out what became of the colonists when we eventually reach the *Persephone*, Mr James."

The aerial view vanished, to be replaced by the jungle immediately outside the smallship. Already it had changed since we last looked out, just minutes before: fresh, budding plant life had replaced the old, and new, bigger and more gorgeous flowers were thrusting their phallic stamens towards the sun.

"We will rendezvous in the hold within the hour," Vakhodia said. "The ship's AI has plotted an optimum route to the *Persephone*, and loaded it into its subsidiary smartcore aboard the crawler. Mr Šarović," he said, and swept from the bridge with his bodyguard hurrying in his wake.

Octavia was tapping her chin as she stared out at the jungle, lost in thought.

"Okay," she said at last. "Hear me out. I'm thinking aloud here." She turned and sat on the handrail, staring at me. "I reckon Vakhodia's lying, that he doesn't have the backing of the USO. I think this is a private mission, and therefore illegal. That would explain why we came down so far away from the starship."

"How so?"

"The USO put a satellite in orbit around Pharantara a couple of months after we left the planet and made our report, right?"

I nodded.

"That satellite was full of surveillance smartware primed to detect any invasive activity on the planet or in orbit around it, principally the ionisation trails made by smallships. My theory is that Vakhodia ordered the AI to bring us down on the blindside of the satellite. Then we landed as close to the *Persephone* as we could without being detected – any closer and the satellite would've picked us up. That's why we're going the rest of the way in the crawler – Vakhodia doesn't want to risk the ship being detected and his presence discovered by the USO."

I thought it through. "And yet he hired the Telemass Organisation to beam us into orbit around the planet."

She shrugged. "He could have a dozen explanations for the transfer," he said. "Maybe he claimed he was on some kind of stellar exploration mission, investigating Arcturus?"

"I wonder…" I said.

"What?"

I commanded my imp to attempt communication with the smallship's AI, then told Octavia what I was doing.

She shook her head. "Don't you think I've already tried that? Nothing doing."

My imp spoke in my head: *The intelligence running the ship is incommunicado. Also, it is employing security baffles to repel communication protocols.*

"You're right," I said to Octavia.

"Which in my book, Jon, suggests that Vakhodia is definitely hiding something."

I gazed out at the writhing jungle. "So," I said at last, "where does that leave us?"

"At the mercy of Mr Vakhodia and the appalling Šarović."

"Am I glad I insisted that you come along for the ride," I said.

"Some ride, Mr James," she said. "You owe me one."

We joined Vakhodia and Šarović in the hold.

The crawler was a state-of-the-art Buffalo with titanium tracks, triple glazed toughened windscreens, and thermostatically controlled air-conditioning. It had a control cabin set high in its forehead, a plush passenger lounge, three small cabins where we would sleep, and a medical bay. The cabin Octavia and I would share provided somewhere to get away from Vakhodia and Šarović when the claustrophobic confines of the crawler became too much. Stent had a berth all to himself in a cargo area to the rear of the vehicle.

I had brought along a carricase of clothing and provisions, a coolsuit and memory-armour. The crawler was stocked with an arsenal of weaponry: laser rifles, stunners and handguns.

Vakhodia informed us that the smallship's AI system would be in control of the crawler, for which I was grateful: I had no desire to take a turn at the controls through such gruelling terrain.

Octavia and I stowed our bags in the crawler's cabin, then moved to the passenger section of the vehicle where Vakhodia was in the process of climbing into the cab above the crawler's snub nose. He invited us to join him.

"Šarović and the Voronian?" Octavia asked as we strapped ourselves in and the AI started the engine.

"Šarović is in his cabin," he said, "and Stent is there."

He pointed through the windscreen. The bulky, armoured alien, wearing nothing but a tabard with a laser rifle slung over his shoulder, was standing before the outer door of the cargo hold.

"What on earth is he doing?" Octavia asked.

"You'll see," Vakhodia replied cryptically.

The great door hinged open and the ramp slowly lowered. The jungle thrashed beyond, a mass of squirming plant-life bathed in the fiery glow of the red giant. The sun was low to the east now, and setting: the twilight would last for a few hours yet, and night itself for a further twenty.

As we watched, the Voronian trundled like some upright rhinoceros down the ramp and into the jungle, sweeping his rifle right and left so that its blue beam scythed through the vegetation before the ramp.

Then the alien set off away from the smallship, mowing down the writhing undergrowth as he went.

"Is he insane?" Octavia asked, incredulous.

Vakhodia smiled. "He's been anticipating this ever since I planned the mission," he said. "The world he comes from, Voronia, makes Pharantara seem like paradise. It's a volcanic planet, and the natives make their homes in caves in the fumaroles of the less active volcanoes. They hunt beasts that translate as 'fire-tigers' across the burn plains. For Stent, this is a walk in the park."

The crawler kicked into life and moved down the ramp, jolting us, and followed the track the Voronian had cleared through the jungle.

I watched the alien, fascinated. To date, I had only ever seen him move with ponderous deliberation, like some pachyderm on barbiturates. Now, in his element, he lumbered along at a fair clip, barrelling through the undergrowth and lasering everything before him.

We bucketed along in his wake, the great titanium tracks of the crawler making light work of the charred vegetation.

I said, "I fear for him if – or rather when – he comes across some of the hostile wildlife out there."

"Don't bother," Vakhodia said. "We studied your report, Mr James, and Stent assured me that he will be equal to anything that Pharantara can throw at him. His tegument is like armour and, as you can see, for his bulk he's deceptively swift on his hooves."

According to the speedometer on the dashboard, we were moving at a little over ten kilometres an hour. A screen showed an aerial view of the southern continent, the mountain range towards which we were heading, and our projected course which was displayed as a flashing dotted line. The crawler showed as a steady red light, hardly moving in relation to the hundred and three kilometres we had yet to travel. The estimated duration of our journey was displayed at the top of the screen: ten hours and thirty-three minutes.

Octavia unstrapped herself, left the cab, and came back with three canisters of ice-cold water. The interior of the vehicle felt chilly thanks to the air-conditioning, but nevertheless I was thirsty just watching the Voronian scythe his way through the sweltering cauldron of the jungle.

I took a long drink, then turned to Vakhodia. "So far," I said, "it seems I'm along merely for the ride. You hired me as a guide, but I'm hardly doing any of that at the moment."

"I hired you for your expertise, Mr James, for your experience of this planet. There is no telling when what you know about Pharantara might be of use. If I have learned nothing else, I know that it is wise to surround myself with people of varying specialisms. You have been to Pharantara: you survived. You are – you, Ms Carrera and the two others of your crew – therefore unique amongst the human race. It made eminent good sense, to me, to hire your services." He gestured to the alien beyond the windscreen. "Of course," he went on, "you could always join Stent for a shift out there."

I fell silent and drank my water.

So far – thanks to the services the AI and the Voronian – he was faring very well without me. Therefore, I could only have been brought along for what I knew of the Pharan themselves.

Their secret.

But how, I asked myself, might Vakhodia know anything about that?

I concentrated on the scene outside the crawler.

We were travelling through an aqueous twilight created by the high canopy of the trees. From time to time, their sturdy trunks barred our way, but Stent's laser was equal to the task. He increased the power of the beam and directed it for five seconds at the intervening tree, which fell in lazy slow motion. If it still barred our way, Stent simply applied a massive shoulder to the trunk and bulldozed it aside.

The Voronian showed no sign of flagging, and I had to admire his endurance.

Here and there I saw plants I recognised from my first time on the planet, and the sight of them brought back a slew of memories: purple bromeliads that hung from branches and whipped up prey in an eye-blink; cilia as tall as a man that were coated in a viscous honey-like slime irresistible to certain wildlife – I had once seen a rodent-analogue as large as a dog come sniffing at the cilia, only to find itself adhering to the strands and drawn, squealing all the way, into the digestive acid of the plant's stomach; things like kites with butterfly wings that folded around unwitting bird-analogues and spooled them to the ground, where a parasitic lizard-analogue lay in wait.

At one point Stent came upon what looked like a glistening pool of oil, fringed with triangular scarlet leaves. We'd almost lost Connor to this monstrosity in the early days of our mission. The fluid exuded a heady, irresistible scent that drew its victims into the grip of the poisonous leaves. Trance-like, Connor had sleepwalked towards the oleaginous pool and bent towards it – saved only by the quick thinking of Lascelles in his wake, who had dragged him away, protesting.

Now, the Voronian gave the growth a wide berth and continued on his way.

Six

Two hours after leaving the smallship, Vakhodia suggested we eat in the passenger lounge behind the cab. He broke out trays of self-heating protein stew and bulbs of iced water. While we ate, Šarović briefly showed himself, taking a tray from the cooler and retreating to his cabin.

Octavia watched him, doing nothing to disguise her contemptuous expression.

When the mercenary had departed, Vakhodia commented, "Barely is the expedition underway, and there is enmity in the camp."

"Is it any wonder?" Octavia said, and described Šarović's earlier behaviour.

"I told him that if he touched me again, he'd regret it."

Vakhodia nodded, his lips pursed. "What one must keep in mind, when dealing with Mr Šarović, is that he hails from the colony world of New Sparta."

"And that excuses his behaviour?" she asked.

Vakhodia tipped his head to one side. "Let's just say that it explains it."

"How so?"

"He was raised in a military crèche and indentured to a mercenary cadre at the age of twelve. From that age he was trained to kill. Drilled into him was obedience to his pay-master. He has none of the finer social graces to be found in the rest of the human race. He is, I regret to say, a barbarian. But, it must be said, a useful one to have around in certain situations."

"So I was rash in threatening him?"

"You would be rash in attempting to get the better of him," he said diplomatically. "I had a little word with him earlier, after the contretemps on the bridge –"

"He told you about it?" I asked.

Vakhodia shook his head. "The scene was relayed to me by the AI," he said. "I told Šarović to ignore you, which he is doing. I could of course have asked him to watch his manners and treat you with respect, but I fear that respect of others is somewhat low on his list of priorities."

We fell silent, and I exchanged a glance with Octavia. From her minimal nod of acknowledgement, I knew she'd taken the salient point from what he'd said: not so much that Šarović was a sub-human killing machine, but that the AI was all-seeing and reported back to Vakhodia.

After the meal, Octavia said she was tired and went to lie down. Vakhodia returned to the cab, and after a while I took another container of water from the cooler and joined him.

The Voronian was still out there, maintaining a steady, indefatigable pace and scything down the vegetation with regular sweeping motions of his laser.

Occasionally the huge, baleful eye of Arcturus showed through the jungle canopy, burning like an ember. It was hard to credit that it was still not yet high summer on Pharantara; that was another six months away, when the planet would be at its closest point to the fiery primary and the mean temperature would soar to one hundred and eighty degrees. Life on the surface of the planet would be impossible for all but a few incredibly hardy and adapted species. I had learned from Tan'lo that in high summer his people retreated to a system of vast caverns many kilometres underground, where they lived until they emerged at the end of summer and remained aboveground for another two or three years as winter approached. Then, as the ice encroached from north and south, and the temperature plummeted to one hundred degrees below zero, they retreated once again en masse to the subterranean caverns, taking with them sufficient plants and livestock to sustain them for ten years until once again spring visited the planet. In lean years, when they had been unable to gather enough edible vegetation and had consumed all the meat, they resorted to scraping an edible but foul tasting fungus from the walls of the caverns. When spring arrived at last, great celebrations were held and the Pharan left their winter fastness and emerged joyously into the sunlight. And so the cycle went on, generation after generation, punishing summer after cruel winter, times of brief plenty alternating with times of scarcity. It was the way of the Pharan, and they gave thanks.

Vakhodia broke into my thoughts.

"You had a distinguished career with the Taurus Line, before Pharantara and your retirement, Mr James."

Nettled by the inference that that career had ended less than gloriously, I considered responding that his statement had not been a question. Instead I said, "Some might say that, yes."

"You do yourself an injustice, my friend. By any standards, you did well. Grades in the top five per cent at cadet college, and commanding a Lunar tug by the age of twenty-five. And that was before you exceeded all expectations and were accepted by the exploratory arm of the Taurus Line."

I smiled at that. "All expectations, yes. Including my own. Hardly anyone moved on from running the tugs between Lagrange and Lunar – it was a dead-end job. It was a pity my father didn't live to see me graduate and fly my first exploratory mission."

"To Spica," he said.

"You've done your research."

He turned a thin hand in a complacent gesture. "I like to know the background of those I hire. You and your team discovered two habitable planets in that system," he went on. "It must be quite a sensation, to step on soil hitherto untrodden by human beings."

"On the first few occasions, yes, it is. But as is the way of things, familiarity breeds – not contempt, but apathy. Repetition tends to dull one's appreciation. Except on those planets which present some feature so extraordinary as to be exceptional."

"For example?"

"Congrieve, Fomalhaut XIV. The equatorial methane falls. It's quite a sight, with the seven moons casting their light on a mile-high drop of liquid methane. And I'll never forget the million-plus herds of yak-analogues on the ice caps of Zakynthos, Groombridge V."

"But you never discovered sentient life, until coming here?"

I took a drink of water. "That's right. I didn't."

"That alone is quite an achievement, Mr James."

"Once in a lifetime," I said.

"Of course, it cannot have offset the tragedy of losing a colleague…"

He let the statement hang, and I wondered how much he knew about the death of Solange Delacroix. Was he privy the confidential report I had made of the incident for the Taurus Line? Only myself, Octavia, and the two other members of my team – plus the high-ups of the Line – knew what had happened here three years ago. The possibility that someone like Santor Vakhodia had read of my lover's death, and my part in it, made me more than a little uneasy.

He murmured, "What happened, Mr James?"

I stared through the windscreen as the crawler trundled through the jungle. I shrugged. "We were on a routine mission to collect botanical samples, Lieutenant Delacroix and I. The long and the short of it is, she succumbed to an attack."

I fell silent and took another drink.

"An animal?"

"A venomous plant, as it happens," I snapped.

"And there was nothing you could have done to save her?"

I stared at him. He was gazing serenely through the windscreen. His questioning was insensitive enough anyway, but

45

as he knew that Solange had been my lover, his curiosity bordered on the sadistic.

I said nothing.

The silence stretched. At last he said, "I heard rumours, Mr James, that you became close to the natives of Pharantara."

I disliked the way he loaded his words; how behind his every statement was the suggestion that he knew far more than he was saying.

"That was inevitable in the circumstance," I said.

"Inevitable? And yet you could not communicate with them, could you? Your implant tech was insufficient to translate, I take it?"

I considered my reply. He must have known that imp technology was capable, after some time, of decoding language and offering a translation. Or did his pleading ignorance suggest that he knew more? Was he aware, in fact, of the secret of the Pharan, which Octavia and I had agreed never to tell anyone, not even our superiors at the Taurus Line?

I said, "My tech could make a rudimentary translation. But even if it couldn't, one can still empathise with an alien race. We had similarities in common: they are hunter-gathers, with an animist belief system and a hierarchical family-tribal structure."

He seemed satisfied with this, and nodded to himself.

As I stared into the enclosing jungle, I wondered if our passage was being observed by the aliens. It had taken a while – over a week – before the Pharan had deigned to show themselves three years ago, yet they had been watching us for that long without our suspecting their presence. They haunted the jungle like ghosts, were adept hunters who could stalk their prey in silence, as if invisible: our blunted human senses had registered nothing, even when they had been mere metres away.

And all the time they had been assessing us.

Now I tried to discern their presence between the trees, behind the vines and lianas out there. I wanted to look upon their slight, timorous forms again; more, I wanted to communicate with the extraordinary aliens.

At the same time, I feared contact between the Pharan and Santor Vakhodia.

For the next half an hour I deflected his questions about that fateful last mission and told him of the many other worlds I'd explored over the course of my thirty years with the Taurus Line.

Later, after I'd replenished our water, I resumed my seat beside him and said, "And you?"

"Me?" he said disingenuously.

"I've given you a stripped-down account of my life, Mr Vakhodia, yet I know nothing about you."

"My life, when compared to yours, with your many adventures, is signally dull and uninspiring."

He was an enigma. He spoke English with an accent I could not place, and his diction was prim, almost archaic. He appeared to be in his forties, yet his skin had the translucent pallor of someone who had undergone the rejuvenation process. As for his origins... He might have hailed from any one of a hundred colony worlds: his slight, bird-like form, his deathly complexion, suggested that he was from some low gravity word far from its sun, but I could easily have been very wrong.

I said, "You're from one of the colonies?"

"I was born on Earth, Mr James. In the state of Greater Europe, though my ancestors hailed from a small country once known as Armenia."

"And your wealth is inherited?"

If I had hoped to nettle him, he did not rise to the ploy. "I came into a fortune, on my eighteenth birthday, amassed by my forbears from mining operations in the Kuiper Belt, as I have previously mentioned." He shot me a glance. "If you think my existence a bed of roses, then think again. It is one thing to inherit wealth, and quite another to nurture that wealth, watch it grow and husband one's resources in such a way that benefits not just myself but those who rely on the success of Vakhodia

Enterprises; hundreds of thousands of them across the Expansion. Over the decades I have expanded my empire in ways that would make the founder proud."

"And this quest for your ancestor aboard the *Persephone?*"

He flicked me a quick glance. "What of it?"

"You said you wish to thank your great-great-great grandfather, face to face. To thank him – and perhaps to earn his praise at what you have made of his initial endeavours?" I ventured. "From a business dealing across the solar system, to one that has grown throughout the entirety of the human Expansion."

"You could say that, yes. He would be... he *will* be... surprised, to say the least."

We fell silent and watched the Voronian surging through the jungle. He had been out there for over four hours without so much as a short break to recoup his strength or to take on water. The alien was a powerhouse of relentless muscle, an armoured slab more mechanical than biological, bent on his thankless task without let or hindrance.

At one point I found myself murmuring, "Remarkable."

Vakhodia smiled. "Only in relation to what our puny selves might manage, Mr James. Compared to his homeworld, this is as nothing. We could not survive one minute on Voronia, even though we could breathe its atmosphere. The heat and humidity would prostrate us in seconds."

"How did he come to work for you?"

"My company employs Voronian overseers in mines on a number of worlds in the Bellatrix system. Stent was brought to my attention as a ceaseless worker and loyal company member. It so happened that I required a being with his attributes."

I gestured at the toiling alien. "To clear the way on Arcturus Seven?"

"You might have noticed the effect of his pheromones," he said. "When a Voronian senses danger, they can instantaneously increase its production, and its potency, and so prevent the attack of an assailant within seconds. They make exceptional bodyguards."

"And yet you and Šarović seem to be unaffected by its presence?"

"We administer ourselves with a daily injection of a serum that renders us immune to the effects."

"All things considered, a handy fellow to have around," I said, noting the alien's attribute should I ever find myself wishing to do harm to Vakhodia in its presence.

"Quite."

I was about to leave the cab and find Octavia, when Vakhodia leaned forward suddenly and stared through the windscreen.

"What?" I said, my pulse surging.

I stared into the jungle, but there was no sign of the Voronian – though his laser rifle lay on the ground five metres before the crawler.

He pointed. "He was there, to the left, just a second ago. I saw—"

"What?" I snapped.

"Something whipped out from the undergrowth and... and then he wasn't there."

"Did you see exactly what –?"

"I didn't see anything... Just a blur."

Vakhodia gave a command. The crawler slowed and jerked to a halt as we came alongside where the Voronian had disappeared. I stared to our left, and saw it.

"Oh, Christ," I said.

Stent was pinned to the bole of a great bloated tuber twice the height of a man, his bulk lashed to the putrescent tegument of the plant by a dozen suckered vines.

The alien struggled as we watched, but even his phenomenal strength was unequal to the task of freeing himself.

I had seen just such a monster, three years ago.

It was the same plant that had captured and killed my lover, Solange Delacroix.

49

Seven

"What are you doing?" Vakhodia barked.

I unbuckled myself and quit the cab. "What the hell do you think?"

I ran through the passenger lounge and down the corridor. Octavia was sitting on her berth, bleary-eyed. "We've stopped –"

"It's got Stent," I said.

"What has?"

I could hardly bring myself to speak its name. "What did the Pharan called them? Khata? I'm going out there."

"Jon?" Octavia said, staring at me.

"I've got to do this."

I rooted around in my carricase and found the memory armour. I slapped it to my chest and felt it flow over and around my coolsuit, encasing my torso and rising to protect my head like a balaclava.

I turned and ran back to the lounge, grabbing a laser rifle and a handgun from the rack.

Octavia was behind me, having donned her armour. "I'm coming with you."

I didn't argue. Vakhodia stood by the door to the cab, his usually impassive face drawn into lines of concern. "Are you sure –?"

"I've experienced those things," I said, checking the laser's charges. "I know Stent is strong, but it's only a matter of time before the khata finds a weak spot. Then he's dead."

Octavia said, "Where's Šarović?"

On cue, the mercenary emerged from his cabin and regarded us. "What gives?"

Vakhodia said, "An alien... *thing*... has captured Stent."

"You're coming with us," Octavia said to Šarović. "We'll cover each other while Jon tackles the khata –"

I interrupted, staring at the mercenary. "Don't fire at it – that'll only make it tighten its grip." I made for the sliding door. "You two cover each other. We don't know what else might be out there. When a khata feeds, it draws predators from all around, attracted by what it discards."

Šarović silently commanded his camouflaged suit, and vanished.

Grabbing a pair of lasers from the rack, Octavia cried at him, "No! For Chrissake, I need to see you out there! How the hell can I cover you if you're invisible?"

Cowed, Šarović reappeared. He took a rifle from the rack and followed Octavia.

Vakhodia said, "How long before Stent –?"

Solange had lasted just minutes, three years ago, before the khata located the seam between her armour at the base of her neck and inserted its poison spike.

"Five minutes, maybe a little more," I said.

Trying not to dwell on what might lie ahead, I hit the control and the door slid silently open.

The heat hammered into me with the force of a blow, almost stopping me in my tracks. The humidity clogged my airways like something solid, a warm soggy sponge. With a sensation of drowning I recalled so well, I staggered from the crawler, my coolsuit labouring to keep my body temperature within acceptable parameters.

Along with the heat and humidity, and the lances of light piercing the high canopy, I was assailed by a cacophony of eerie jungle sounds. The pulsing, bassoon throb of a giant frog-analogue was like a constant heartbeat, overlaid by the shrill keening of a dozen arboreal creatures.

Already the avenue through the undergrowth, trampled minutes earlier by Stent as he was dragged off by the khata, had been filled by growing things, twining bindweed and dependent vines.

Raising my lasers, I cut my way through the vegetation towards where the Voronian was imprisoned.

I was aware of Octavia and Šarović to my right and left, their lasers levelled.

I stopped when I saw the khata, five metres before us, and was overtaken by a flood of memories I did my best to suppress.

Stent had ceased struggling. At first I thought the poison had killed him – then I saw his open eyes, staring at me. I chose to read desperation, and hope, in his alien expression. He had realised the futility of fighting against the encompassing tentacles – to do so had only drawn them ever tighter around him. He had ceased his struggles and, perhaps for the first time in his life, placed his trust in others.

Then I heard a sound that made me gag – the metallic tapping of the khata's venomous spikes as they probed the Voronian's toughened hide for a weak spot.

Thanks to the Pharan, I knew how to combat the khata.

I advanced over ground made spongy by a thick layer of compost – the accreted, rotted remains of the khata's previous victims – raised my laser and traced the tentacle that connected the crown of the khata to the bough of its parent tree high overhead.

Then, before I could fire, something screamed to my right and knocked me off my feet.

A man-trap of hideous fangs closed around my torso, biting down on my body armour. I yelled out. Octavia fired. Her beam pierced the monster's head which exploded in a noxious spew of liquefied brain. Gagging, I staggered to my feet.

"You okay?" she called out.

"Cover me!" I ordered as I raised my laser once again, took aim at the junction of tentacle and bough high overhead, and fired.

The beam connected with the goitre and the tentacle dropped, missing me by inches. Instantly, the tentacles around Stent's bulk loosened their grip and he surged forward with a roar, lashing out at his erstwhile binds and staggering towards us.

I retched, overcome by nausea as the Voronian came within range, a dizzying desire to fall flat on my face and vomit. Like a charging rhino, Stent barrelled through the undergrowth towards us, then changed his course when he saw the effect he was having on Octavia and myself. He veered to our left, charging towards the crawler, and instantly my nausea lifted.

Šarović, to his credit, covered us like a professional as we staggered back to the vehicle.

The door slid open and the Voronian bounded inside, followed by Šarović. Octavia waited, covering me as I approached the crawler and leapt into the chill of the lounge.

I leaned against the wall, breathing hard, then looked over my shoulder expecting to see Octavia.

She wasn't there.

Heart thumping, I stepped outside and called her name.

She appeared form my right, smiling. "It's fine, Jon. Just tripped up on the way back."

Relieved, I grabbed her arm and helped her into the crawler, and the door sighed shut behind us.

I collapsed on a lounger and punched my chest, and the armour withdrew. Octavia hauled open the cooler and passed containers of water to me and Šarović. I drank like someone dying of thirst, then poured water over my head.

The Voronian stood at the far end of the lounge, two stubby arms braced against the wall, its head hanging.

Octavia snapped, "Get him to the med-bay!"

Between Šarović and Vakhodia, they manhandled the alien's bulk along the corridor away from us. Octavia followed at a distance.

I finished my water and sat for a while, eyes closed as I relived what had happened out there. Then I re-racked the lasers, moved to my cabin and lay face down on the bunk.

I heard Solange's dying screams again, her pleading with me to do something. The tragedy was that it would have been so easy to have saved her life back then.

I heard the door swish open and Octavia entered. She sat on the bunk facing mine, her elbows lodged on her knees.

She said, "You okay, Jon?"

"I'm fine. I've had years to..." I shrugged, then smiled. "It feels good to have got one over on that thing, you know? How's Stent?"

"The khata injected him, despite his armoured hide."

"That would've been enough to kill you or me outright."

"The AI medic's put him into an induced coma. It's treating him with some serum."

"Maybe we weren't quick enough."

"We'll see."

I gestured through the wall of the crawler. "Good shot out there," I said.

She shrugged. "I never saw it coming. I swear I was watching you, but it came on my blindside."

"What the hell was it?"

"The Pharan call them ghen, which means simply 'teeth'."

I smiled. "Appropriate."

She looked at me, then said in a murmur, "I saw them out there, Jon."

"Them?"

"The Pharan. They were watching us. At least six of them, high in one of the trees. I thought maybe they'd retreated underground by now, but apparently not."

"So they're out there," I said. The thought was at once reassuring and disturbing. While they were watching over us, there was always the chance that Vakhodia or Šarović might make contact with them, accidental or otherwise.

Octavia said, "I wondered if they'd seek us out. But it's best if they don't."

"They're no fools. They'll soon weigh up the situation and keep well away."

She nodded.

I said, "They must know, though."

She peered at me. "Know?"

"About Vakhodia, and whether he's aware of their ability."

"That's possible," she allowed.

"I wonder..." I began.

"Go on."

"If we – you or I – were to make contact–"

She shook her head, vehement. "Too dangerous, Jon. We can't risk Vakhodia finding out." She stopped, then whispered, "The AI. We need to be careful."

A tap sounded at the door, and it slid open. Vakhodia looked from Octavia to me. "He's ill, but he'll pull though. I'm giving the AI the order to continue. We can't wait until Stent is fit enough to go back out there."

I sat up. "You mean you'd send him out there again?"

"Before the AI put him under, Mr James, Stent expressed the wish to continue what he was doing. He said he'd learnt from what happened. It's his duty, after all, to serve."

I exchanged a glance with Octavia, who remained stony faced.

Vakhodia said, "The AI estimates that we should reach the valley in approximately six hours, factoring in our slower pace now that Stent is no longer clearing a way through the undergrowth." As he spoke, the crawler started up, its engines grumbling, and we bucked over the uneven terrain.

Vakhodia gripped the door-frame as the vehicle rocked, then he nodded to us and moved off down the corridor.

When the door slid shut, I murmured, "A word of thanks for what we did out there wouldn't have gone amiss."

Octavia smiled. "People like him don't thank anyone, Jon."

"Not even a simple acknowledgement that we risked our lives?"

"Get real. As far as he's concerned, as he said in relation to Stent, it's our duty to serve."

"I'm dead beat," I said, stretching out on the bunk. "I'm going to get some sleep."

Octavia gestured in the direction of the cab. "I'll join Vakhodia. I want to talk to him."

"About?"

"His mission here," she said. "I want to try to work out how much he knows about the Pharan."

"And good luck with that," I said.

She left the cabin and I turned over and closed my eyes as the crawler started up and trundled through the jungle.

Eight

I was pitched from a deep sleep – literally – when the crawler tipped and I found myself lying on what had been the wall, blinking myself awake and trying to work out what had happened.

From the configuration of the cabin, with Octavia's bunk now above me, it was obvious that the vehicle had pitched forward and was canted at a slope of some eighty degrees.

Whatever damage we might have sustained, at least the structure of the vehicle had not been breached. The air-conditioning was still humming away and there was no suggestion that the heat from outside was entering the crawler.

"Imp," I thought. "How long have I been asleep?"

Five hours and seven minutes, it replied.

"What the hell happened?"

Insufficient data.

I struggled upright and crawled across to the door, which slid open at my touch.

The engine was silent – which was ominous on two counts. Either the crawler had suffered in the accident, and the engine wasn't functioning – or both Octavia and Vakhodia were injured and unable to issue the AI with the command to restart the vehicle.

I peered through the doorway, staring down the well of the corridor to the passenger lounge and the cab. I listened, but detected no sound of movement from within.

I found a series of projections in the corridor wall to use as hand- and foot-holds. I climbed carefully from the cabin and scaled the wall, descending hand over hand.

I reached the lounge and rested, gripping a light-fitting on the ceiling, with my feet lodged on the edge of the cooler.

As I balanced there, regaining my breath, the engine surged into life and the crawler pitched forward with a sudden jerk, almost dislodging me. I swung out but held on, trusting that someone had given the command to start the engine, and the AI wasn't using its own initiative. I just hope that that someone was Octavia.

Then the crawler juddered as the tracks attempted to gain purchase on the slope, and failed. We remained where we had been, vibrating with the power of the engine. More worryingly, I heard a high-pitched whine followed by a loud, rhythmic thrashing sound as one of the tracks snapped and hit something with every revolution.

"Octavia!" I yelled, peering down at the door of the cab.

The engine cut out suddenly, and with it the rhythmic lashing of the sheared track.

The hatch of the cab, below me, swung open like a trapdoor and Octavia appeared, looking up at me. "Jon! You okay?"

"I'm fine. You?"

"We're both okay. Šarović is down here with us, too. The AI said Stent was shaken about a bit, but he'll be fine."

"What the hell happened?"

"Come down and take a look." Her tone carried a grim fatalism.

I planned my route down to the hatch, then moved from projection to projection until I stood on the bulkhead. Octavia was now sitting on the far side of the hatch, her legs dangling into the cab. I knelt, then leaned forward and peered down.

Vakhodia and Šarović hung from what was now the ceiling, strapped into the seats. They appeared comical, pinned in position and staring down with pained expressions. I would have laughed, or at least smiled, if it hadn't been for what I saw through the windscreen.

The nose of the crawler was buried in a bank of soil, the windscreen just inches from a wall of loam and roots. To our left, I made out the silver treads of the crawler's damaged track, concertinaed in a neat pile where it had come adrift and fetched up against the banking.

"What happened?"

"The ground just opened up before us and we pitched into a ravine," Octavia said.

"How deep are we?"

"Not that deep. But the thing is, we don't know how far down it goes. And as you can see" – she gestured through the windscreen – "the track's snapped."

"Worse," Vakhodia said, grimacing as the strap bit into his chest as gravity asserted itself, "the AI reports a negative outcome scenario."

I laughed. "Which is a basic AI euphemism for 'we're stuffed'."

"The crawler cannot get out of the ravine," he assented, "and even if it could, we do not have the means to repair the track."

"Okay," I said, thinking through the situation. "So what's the terrain like around here?"

"That's the first thing I thought of when my head cleared," Octavia said. "I suggested that Vakhodia send out a drone to see if we could have the smallship land nearby." She shook her head. "For the past few hours we've been in the foothills of a mountain range. We're in a valley with no level surface for tens of kilometres."

"Right," I said. "Very well. So how far are we from the *Persephone*?"

She pointed down, between her dangling feet, to the dashboard and the screen. It showed our route into the foothills, and our present position, a flashing red asterisk more than nine-tenths along the route.

"The AI states that we're five kay from the ship, as the crow flies. Seven or eight, given the lie of the land."

"So this is what we do," I said. "Get the AI to plan the safest route – in terms of negotiable terrain – between here and the *Persephone*. Then we load ourselves with provisions and hike."

Vakhodia cast me a fearful glance. "Is that wise?"

"The alternative is that we stay here and eventually starve to death."

"I was thinking that perhaps two of us might make our way to the *Persephone*, assess whether it is equipped with anything like a crawler and, if it is, return here for the others."

"And who might you have in mind for that?" I asked.

He turned his head and stared up at me. "You and me, Mr James," he said.

His reply surprised me. I had been sure he'd elect to remain in the relative safety of the crawler. I wondered what ulterior motive he had in mind.

I said, "You saw what the land was like around the starship. Even if we found a vehicle, we wouldn't be able to negotiate the terrain and get back here. Chances are, even if we hadn't ended up in the ravine, we would have had to cover the last few kilometres on foot anyway."

He considered my words, then said, "So, when we reach the ship? What then?"

"We'll be able to use the crew quarters as a base. Those ships were equipped with emergency food and water rations to cover all eventualities. Once we've established ourselves there, we scout the nearest level land – or construct some kind of landing site ourselves – and call in the smallship. Right, I suggest I get out of here and plot a safe route from the ravine."

Vakhodia said, "After we crashed, I had the AI send out a second drone, bound for the *Persephone*." He indicated the screen in the dashboard. "It's a minute from arriving. We'll be able to tell, perhaps, what awaits us."

Šarović said, "If there were no survivors, Mr Vakhodia..."

Vakhodia turned his head sharply and snapped, "Yes?"

"Then all this... then the entire mission... has been redundant."

"I didn't hear you object when you accepted the generous salary I offered, Mr Šarović."

"I'm not objecting," Šarović said, "merely pointing out an obvious fact."

"Which is hardly helpful in the situation. I am confident that we'll find the colonists either still in coldsleep or, if the *Persephone's* running system was compromised, sheltering in the crew quarters previously mentioned by Mr James."

Šarović scowled and looked away.

Octavia pointed down to the screen.

The schematic of our route had cleared, to be replaced by an aerial view of the broken-backed *Persephone* wedged in the mountain valley. As we watched, the drone transmitting these images lost altitude and approached the ship.

The jungle had crept up the valley and over the vessel's superstructure, covering the curving panels so that in places it was impossible to tell that there was a man-made object beneath the mass of vegetation. The drone descended, approaching the great lateral rent in the mid-section of the ship, slowed down and slipped through the five metre wide gap.

It was a shadowy, twilight world within. I made out a vast chamber with circumferential galleries and lateral walkways criss-crossing the space like cat's cradles. Even here the jungle had invaded, and great vines and lianas hung in swathes, along with trumpeting bromeliads. There was something at once eerie and ominous about the juxtaposition of abundant nature invading such a high-tech environment.

"There's no sign of human life," Octavia murmured beside me.

Vakhodia said, "I instructed the AI to have the drone head first for the crew quarters, and then for the coldsleep chambers."

I glanced at him. He seemed to be holding his breath as he hung there, staring down at the screen.

The moving image dropped, heading towards the rear of the *Persephone* where the crew quarters were situated. Vegetable life proliferated here; every surface was covered – in places it was impossible to tell that this was the interior of a starship.

"Look," Octavia said, pointing.

I made out broken bulkheads and fallen galleries. The drone hovered over the remains of the crew quarters, and it was clear that they were no longer inhabited.

"So," Vakhodia said with desperate hope in his voice, "the colonists must still be in coldsleep."

The drone turned and flew towards the front of the ship.

The screen showed a lateral walkway arrowing into the distance. At the far end I made out the triangular entrance to the coldsleep chamber, twice as tall as man. The sliding hatch was open, which suggested that at least some of the colonists had been resuscitated.

The drone flew into the chamber and paused, hovering. It panned its camera to the right and left, and Vakhodia gasped.

The coldsleep pods were stacked in galleries six high, with perhaps a hundred pods along each level, diminishing in perspective. The drone moved slowly towards the banked pods to the left and flew along the length of the chamber.

The frosted side-panel of every pod was open, and the pods themselves were empty. The drone moved from level to level, relaying the same stark image: row after row of silent, vacant coldsleep pods.

The drone crossed to the other side and repeated its sweep, with the same result. Every pod was open, its erstwhile inhabitant no longer in situ.

The drone accelerated towards a triangular aperture which gave access to the second coldsleep chamber.

To my imp, I thought: "Estimate how many colonists inhabited each chamber."

The reply was almost instant: *One thousand two hundred. In total, the* Persephone *had carried three thousand six hundred colonists.*

I leaned forward, staring down at the screen.

The view was identical to that in the first chamber: gallery after gallery of open, empty coldsleep pods.

"Look!" Šarović said, pointing.

At the far end of the second chamber, where a triangular portal accessed the third, the bulkhead was blackened with fire damage.

The drone accelerated and entered the third chamber, no longer a recognisable coldsleep facility but a crumpled, fire-blackened mass of metal and melted combustible material.

The drone scanned along the buckled deck, and beside me Octavia swore quietly to herself.

The wreckage was strewn with the barely recognisable shapes of the burnt, twisted corpses that had been pitched from their pods into the conflagration.

Vakhodia hung his head and closed his eyes. He didn't have to be told that a third of the colonists had perished upon landing – and who knew how many of those that had survived the initial impact had managed to make it through the two harsh, increasingly hostile years since then?

"So if over two thousand survived landfall," Šarović said, "then where the hell are they?"

Vakhodia ordered the drone to leave the wreckage and scan the land adjacent to the ship.

It retraced its flight from the coldsleep chambers and headed for the glimmering strip of sunlight slanting in through the rent in the superstructure. We watched as it rose, hovered above the ship, and scanned the valley to the east and west.

If the colonists had left the comparative safety of the ship, then they had not set up camp either in the jungle or on the empty, scree covered slopes.

Into the resulting silence, I said, "So we make our way to the ship as planned, and try to determine what happened to the colonists, right?"

Vakhodia said, "I think, upon consideration, that that is the logical course of action."

Beside me, Octavia nodded, and Šarović did not voice any opposition.

"Ideally we'll need Stent with us," I said. "Šarović, could you go and assess whether he's fit enough to leave the med-bay?"

The mercenary looked at Vakhodia, who nodded his assent. Šarović unfastened himself from his seat, climbed past us and scaled the canted passenger lounge.

"And if Stent is unequal to the journey?" Vakhodia asked.

"Then there's nothing for it," I said. "He'll have to remain here. Right, I'm going out there to see how difficult it'll be to climb from the ravine."

"I'll come with you," Octavia said.

"I suggest you gather as many provisions as we can carry," I said to Vakhodia, "along with backpacks, bedrolls, weapons, food and water. It might only be seven kilometres to the ship." I went on, "but it'll be no stroll in the park."

I left them, climbed to the cabin and donned my memory armour, then collected a laser rifle and a handgun and checked their charges.

I opened the sliding door, Octavia at my side. The blast of heat rocked me back on my feet, and the sounds coming from the surrounding jungle were deafening.

I gripped the side of the door and peered out.

Nine

We were due a break, and perhaps this was it.

The crawler's cab hung over an almost vertical drop, but the exit was directly above a patch of sloping ground scraped bare by the vehicle's precipitous slide. I looked up the side of the crawler to the margin of jungle on the lip of the ravine, ten metres above us.

Vakhodia had gathered a pile of water canisters and food trays, and located five backpacks. He was squatting in the well of the sloping lounge, quickly filling the backpacks with provisions.

Šarović appeared above us, climbing down – and I was relieved to see the Voronian behind him, his bulk filling the corridor.

"The AI says he'll be fine," Šarović said. "I suggested he stay behind to recuperate, but he wanted to come with us."

I looked up at Stent, and nodded to him. I was surprised when the Voronian inclined his head in acknowledgement. He remained where he was, his huge body braced at an angle in the corridor, his feet lodged in the doorway of a berth for support. He stared at me, and I wondered if I was deluding myself in thinking I detected gratitude in his gaze for my having saved his life.

We each shouldered a backpack loaded with food and water, along with spare weapons and ammunition. I took a long drink of water, then looked at Vakhodia. "You have a softscreen with the route the AI planned?"

"Here," he said, tapping the chest of his jacket.

"If you could squirt the details to my imp," I said, "it'll save having to stop and refer to the 'screen." I gave him my code.

He pulled out and unrolled his softscreen, and seconds later my imp acknowledged receipt of the cache.

"Overlay," I said.

A map of the immediate terrain, marked with our current position and that of the starship, appeared on my retina. I studied it for a while, then dismissed the overlay.

"Let's go," I said, shouldering the laser rifle and slipping the handgun into my belt.

I climbed to the door and stepped out onto the slope, using the vehicle's aerial mounts and the window recesses as handholds to aid my ascent. When I came to the rear of the crawler, drenched in sweat despite my coolsuit, I looked back to see Octavia and Šarović assisting Vakhodia up the ravine. Stent followed them.

They caught up with me and Vakhodia leaned against the back of the crawler, ashen faced and breathing hard. I wondered how he would fare in the journey ahead, and if Stent might have to carry him at some point. The image made me smile.

I indicated the handgun in his belt. "You used one of those before?"

He shook his head. "Never."

"Keep it drawn with the safety off and directed at the ground. Only use it if I say so, okay? The rest of us are armed and we'll be on the alert for whatever's out there."

He nodded, looking nervous, and allowed himself a brief smile.

The ravine rose above us, a black trench made by the crawler's slide. Above it, jungle loomed, and above the jungle, the burning ember of Arcturus hung on the tree-fringed horizon.

I checked with my imp, which told me that the sun would set in four hours, beginning a twenty hour night.

I relayed this information to the others, and went on, "Sunset in four hours, though it will never get completely dark. We'll stop then, and make camp, taking turns to keep watch while the others sleep."

I could see that Šarović wanted to add something – perhaps he resented my authority – but my interrogative glance silenced him.

I unshouldered my laser and levelled it, then led the way up the slope, scanning ahead. We came to the lip of the ravine and faced an intimidating wall of jungle. I didn't hesitate, but swept the laser in a brief, economical arc, its bright blue beam scything down the undergrowth.

The land rose before us, though it was impossible to make out anything more than a scant three or four metres ahead, such was the density of the vegetation. Added to the heat of the sun, and the sapping humidity, was the heat of the undergrowth as it smouldered under the laser assault, giving off a noxious odour. I checked behind me from time to time, reassured by what I saw. Octavia immediately followed me, scanning to the right. Vakhodia came next, then Šarović, and he kept his attention to our left. Stent brought up the rear, armed with a laser rifle and scanning right and left.

The terrain was treacherous underfoot, and snagged with roots and briars. We high-stepped through the worst of the tangles and were grateful when we reached an extensive area covered by a mat of crimson moss as smooth as velvet and overhung with trees.

The sound of wildlife was constant and often startling. An ever-present bass note was provided by the unseen frog-analogue which called out every three seconds. From time to time something shrieked and cawed like a maniac, causing me to swing and aim my laser in alarm.

There was no sign of the Pharan, for which I was thankful. Octavia had said she'd seen them in the jungle earlier, but I wondered if she'd been mistaken and they'd already migrated underground for the duration of the summer.

I called a break for water every fifteen minutes, and we drank in relays while the non-drinkers stood guard. Then we set off again, climbing steadily towards the setting sun. Occasionally, through the cover high overhead, I caught glimpses of a stark grey mountain range. Somewhere in the folded foothills ahead, the *Persephone* was a stranded mausoleum to the thousand-plus colonist who had perished. And the survivors, I asked myself: had they found refuge somewhere, or succumbed to the predators that haunted the jungle?

After an hour, I was exhausted. A life of retirement, during which the most energetic exercise I ever took was a stroll into the nearby village, had hardly prepared me for the punishing trek. I called another water halt and suggested that Stent and I change positions, with him leading the way while I brought up the rear. He said nothing when I addressed him, but nodded his assent and gave me a wide berth as he took up his position at the head of the column.

We set off again.

From time to time I commanded my imp to overlay the route map, and I'd call ahead if our course needed any adjustment.

"Imp," I thought at one point, "estimated time of arrival at the starship?"

"*Factoring in an eight hour break for sleep, we will arrive at the* Persephone *in approximately eleven hours.*"

I scanned ahead, over the heads of my companions and to their right and left. Every fifteen seconds I turned a full circle, checking the jungle in our wake. All I made out was the smouldering track we had made, with smoke gently rising in the red light of dusk.

I kept a particular lookout for the khata which had captured Stent, peering into the jungle on either side for any sign of the ribbed tree trunks from which the huge seed pods depended. I saw none, and wondered whether I was simply missing them, or they didn't grow at this altitude.

At one point, Šarović called out over his shoulder, "You been on many jungle worlds?"

"I've been to quite a few worlds where there've been jungles," I said, "along with deserts and savannah and forests and ice caps. But I've seen a few jungles in my time, yes."

"You equip yourself like a soldier."

"Basic training," I said.

"You can handle yourself in close combat?"

My suspicion prickled. Why his interest? "We're trained in a number of military situations."

He nodded, continued scanning the jungle to our right.

What if Octavia had been correct in her supposition that Vakhodia was here illegally, I asked myself? What if, at journey's end, Octavia and I were surplus to requirements?

I told myself to concentrate on the job at hand, rather than fill my mind with paranoid speculation.

Up ahead, Octavia called out, grabbed Vakhodia and dragged him to the ground. At the same time, kneeling, she raised her rifle and fired off a quick beam.

The flying creature swooped down on our little group, then screeched and veered as Octavia's laser scorched its leathery wings. It crashed to earth to our right with an ear-piercing scream of pain.

My heart crashing, I approached the creature and stared down at a charred mess of membranous wings, sickle claws, and a beak like that of a pterodactyl. The monster threshed, trying to raise itself and swipe at us with its scimitar beak. Octavia stepped forward and finished it off with a quick beam to its head.

Vakhodia picked himself up and dusted himself down with a shaking hand. I was heartened to see that Stent and Šarović had taken up defensive positions, right and left, while Octavia had attended to the creature.

"I never saw it coming," Vakhodia said, clearly in shock.

"You often don't," Octavia said, "until it's too late."

"Let's get going," I said, "before the smell of its meat attracts scavengers. We'll walk for another hour, then make camp for the night."

We set off again.

The huge sun was no longer visible through the treetops. Its slow setting had brought down a bloody twilight and caused a diminution in the chorus of animal noises. Only the ever-present, repetitive booming sounded, like the heartbeat of the planet. Also, the heat dropped by a few degrees, though if anything the humidity increased. My face ran with sweat, despite my coolsuit, and the constricting body armour was growing uncomfortable.

The thought of ice-cold water, and food, spurred me on.

A little before I had planned to call a halt for the night, we came to an outcropping of silver rock that jutted from the jungle. We stopped and I looked ahead, judging that the wall of rock extended for half a kilometre.

Octavia agreed with me that this was a near ideal place to call a halt, with the wall of rock providing cover for our backs. We burned a semi-circular area in the undergrowth, some five metres deep, before the outcropping.

I suggested that Vakhodia and Šarović take the first four hour sleep period, and Octavia and myself the second.

Vakhodia said, "Voronians sleep for a period of two hours approximately once a week, Mr James. He'll remain awake for the next three days."

He and Šarović ate in silence, and then Šarović and Stent guarded us while Octavia and I ate our rations. I removed my body armour, luxuriating in the sense of release for ten minutes, then resumed the armour and took up my lasers.

"I was wondering," Vakhodia said as he prepared his bedroll in the lee of the rock, "what might have happened to the surviving colonists? Why might they have left the relative safety of the ship?"

I hesitated, looking at Octavia. "I think we might find out when we reach the Persephone, Mr Vakhodia. It's futile to speculate until then."

He nodded, lay down and closed his eyes.

Stent moved off further down the rock wall, and took up a position staring into the jungle. Octavia and I sat cross-legged before Vakhodia and Šarović, lasers at the ready. Ahead of us, over the jungle canopy, a scatter of stars appeared in the indigo heavens.

When I heard the combined snoring of the sleeping men, I moved closer to Octavia and told her what Šarović had asked me about my combat training. "It was as if he was trying to asses me," I said. "If you're right, and Vakhodia and his henchmen are here illegally, then you and me are the only people who could get word back to the USO."

"The same thought occurred to me," she murmured.

"Vakhodia himself is no threat. But Šarović is dangerous, and so is Stent. I'm sure the Voronian's hide would withstand a laser beam, so if he's ordered to attack us…"

"We're safe enough until Vakhodia gets what he wants, Jon. After that, we need to be very careful."

"Agreed."

I broke out more water and passed her a container. We drank.

After a while, she said, "This reminds me of Mantissa," she said, pointing up at the night sky. "The pulsing stars, the view from the shore as Fomalhaut set in the ocean. We had a great leave there, didn't we?"

I looked at her. Mantissa was where Octavia had met Garcia. I recalled asking about him back on Néos Kyrenia, and how she'd been cagey with her reply.

I said, "So how is it with you and Garcia?"

She shrugged, then said, "It's over, Jon. He left six months ago. Walked out. Said we'd grown apart over the years, become different people. He said he didn't like me being away for long shifts. Fact was, he didn't like me being stronger than him. Often happens."

"I'm sorry."

She shrugged. "I was cut up back then, but time heals everything." She hesitated, then asked, "Has there been anyone since Solange?"

"I'm too old, too set in my ways. I'm happy on the island, just seeing friends." It was true, I told myself, and it was to Octavia's credit that she didn't try to persuade me otherwise.

"You know, I still miss her, Jon. She was a good person. Hell," she went on, "I never thought we'd be back here one day."

"You're not the only one —"

I stopped.

"What is it?"

"My God," I said.

Octavia leapt to her feet, swinging her laser. "You're frightening me, Jon!"

"They're here."

She stared at me quickly, then turned her attention back to the shadowy jungle. "The Pharan?"

"The Pharan."

I couldn't see them, of course: the Pharan were far too clever, and careful, to allow themselves to be observed by humans if they wanted to remain unseen. But they were there, in the jungle, watching us.

I could *feel* them...

Three years ago, they had made themselves known to us in this very fashion — after they had observed me and my team for a week and come to the conclusion that we were no threat.

They had called out to me, mind to mind.

I recalled the very first time it had happened, and my initial confusion, followed by wonder. It had felt like a tickle in the back brain — starting like the sensation one sometimes has of knowing you have forgotten something, but cannot recall what.

I had heard a definite voice, beckoning me. *Jonathan... Jonathan...*

I had been in the jungle with Octavia at the time. Solange, Connor and Lascelles had been back at the ship, taking time out.

The voice had called my name, over and over.

Just when I thought I was going mad, Octavia had turned to me and stared, open-mouthed. She had heard it too, the calling of *her* name.

"What the...?" I said.

They had drawn us, siren like, through the jungle to what I can only describe as a nest, a communal cocoon of ferns and feathery leaves, where fifty of their people temporarily dwelled, and then they had spoken to us, mind to mind.

For a week they had studied us, read our minds, gained an understanding of our language. Then they had communicated with us, introduced themselves as the Pharan of the world they called Pharantara, an ancient people who had risen to sentience almost half a million years ago, Terran reckoning, and existed in equilibrium with their harsh environment of blisteringly hot summers and frozen winters.

They had lured Octavia and me further into the jungle and given us their secret – the fact that they were a telepathic hive-mind, the first that humankind had discovered in its outward push through the universe.

And Octavia and I knew instantly what we had to do... or rather what we had *not* to do.

We could tell no one, not even the other members of our team, about the telepathic Pharan. If the USO became wise to their existence, then the way of life the aliens had known for half a million years would come to an end – and, who knows, the Pharan too. For humanity would stop at nothing, Octavia and I reasoned, to discover the physiological basis of their telepathy. We foresaw a time when our scientists would study the extraterrestrials as they would laboratory animals, dissecting their brains in a bid to learn their secret.

So at mission's end we had reported to our superiors that we had discovered a sentient hunter-gather race, rated as B3 on the Mannheim Scale of cultural development – which meant that Pharantara was now out of bounds to human traffic. Satellite monitors would be placed in orbit above the world, and the

Pharan would be left to continue their lives in peace, while humankind's scientists and xenologists devoted their attention to the hundred other alien races in the teeming galaxy.

For the time being, at least.

I had met with the Pharan who called himself Tan'lo, and explained our decision to him – why we would not tell our superiors of the aliens' unique ability.

He – and by extension his people, for they were in effect one great gestalt being – found it almost impossible to comprehend the threat posed by humankind. They saw the images in my mind, no doubt, but perhaps assumed I was deluded. For while they lived in a hostile world, they could not conceive of a *sentient* race that might dominate, or subjugate, or harm, another. I had pleaded with him that if ever a follow-up mission came to their world, they were to avoid it, and under no circumstance make contact and tell its members of their race's telepathic ability.

I sensed their scepticism, and pleaded with them to do as I bid.

I had left that penultimate meeting not at all sure they would heed my words.

I had just one further meeting with the Pharan, a week later, when Solange met her death.

Ten

Octavia whispered, "They want you to go to them, Jon."

I looked to my left, to where the Voronian stood like a monolith. He was facing the jungle with his back to us.

She murmured, "Go. I'll keep guard here."

"What might they want?"

She pushed me. "There's only one way to find out."

My heart was hammering. I recalled the sensation of meeting the Pharan three years ago, the overwhelming knowledge of my privileged experience and the fact that I was communicating telepathically with an alien race.

Ensuring that Stent did not see me, I crept forward into the margin of the jungle, following the siren-call of the Pharan in my mind.

I passed from starlight into the gloom of the jungle cover, treading carefully, peering ahead for the first sign of the tiny aliens.

Then I felt words form in my head: *You are safe, Jonathan. Come to us...*

And I knew I could trust their declaration. When we had first met, I'd been wary of allowing the unique situation of our contact to put me off my guard, but they had reassured me. I had no need to be alert to the danger of predators, for with their telepathic ability they had quelled the ravenous beasts in the vicinity, created what amounted to an exclusion zone in which we could converse in complete safety.

Now I relaxed, confident with their reassurance.

I saw the first Pharan, standing before me, staring: he drew me on with a motion of both hands towards his chest, then turned and slipped like a wraith through the shadows. I followed.

Soon I came to a woven nest in the undergrowth where fifty or so of his kind had created a temporary dwelling, and I sat cross-legged amongst them and opened my mind to their gestalt being.

I was in a daze. Time had no meaning, or relevance. I had no idea how long I remained there, listening to what they had to tell me. I felt as if I were drugged, and experienced a soporific languor that I realised – only later – anaesthetised me to the shock of their subsequent warning.

"*Jonathan,*" they spoke as one in my head. "*Welcome again to Pharantara. We greet you.*"

I thought greetings at them, and my delight at being accepted.

"*We have dwelled in the minds of your human companions, Jonathan,*" they said.

"Vakhodia and Stent," I returned.

"*We have dwelled in the mind of the individual who calls himself Santor Vakhodia.*"

"And?" I asked, fearing their reply.

"*We have seen what you term 'evil' there, and know now as true what you told us, those many sunrises ago. Your race does have individuals who nourish evil thoughts, for wholly selfish reasons, and Santor Vakhodia is one such.*"

"Tell me," I thought.

"*Santor Vakhodia desires your death, and Octavia's, and will order it, when you have helped him achieve what he desires.*"

I experienced a quick surge of dread. "Which is?"

"*Contact with the people who came here in their great ship, many sunrises ago.*"

I leaned forward. "They are safe?"

"*We have led them to safety, Jonathan. But,*" they went on, "*Santor Vakhodia desires to commit evil when he makes contact with these people – for his motives are not what he has led you to believe.*"

76

"Please, tell me."

"*He does not wish to make contact with an ancestor, as he told you, but with a woman called Anna Kallinova. And when he does meet her, he will do her harm, kill her.*" I sensed, in their minds, their abhorrence as they transmitted the fact.

Their thoughts were interrupted by a wave of alarm that swept through the gathering.

"*He is coming, the creature you call Stent. He has heard noises, and is approaching. We must go before he discovers us. Hurry, Jonathan, and heed our words – Santor Vakhodia wishes you ill.*"

The mind contact ceased suddenly, leaving a ringing silence in my head. The aliens ranged before me slipped away, moved silently from their makeshift nest, and within seconds had vanished.

I rose to my feet and staggered from the nest, incoherently thanking them as I went. I was numbed with the soporific effect of the mind-communion, dazed with what I'd learned and the thought of what lay ahead.

I heard a sound to my right, the lumbering of the Voronian through the undergrowth. I moved to my left, away from Stent, and hurried through the jungle before he found me.

I came to the clearing minutes later and hurried across to Octavia.

"Jon?" she said, taking my shoulders in both hands and shaking me.

Behind her, Vakhodia was stirring. He sat up in the starlight, staring across at him. "What...?" he said groggily.

Octavia turned to him. "Go back to sleep. It's not your turn to stand watch yet."

He settled down again, turned over and lay with his back to us.

I stared at him, a part of me wanting to laser him dead while he slept.

I pulled Octavia along the length of the outcropping until we were well out of earshot, then sat down with my back against the rock. Octavia sat cross-legged before me, her face etched with concern.

To our left, Stent emerged from the jungle and took up his sentry position beyond the sleeping forms of Vakhodia and Šarović.

I said, "The Pharan told me that Vakhodia will kill us when he gets what he wants. And all that talk about contacting his ancestor – it's a lie."

"What?"

"The Pharan say he plans to kill a woman called Anna Kallinova – and then he intends to kill you and me once he finds her."

"Kill her? But why? Why the hell does Vakhodia want to kill Kallinova?"

"The Pharan didn't say – we were interrupted by Stent. They just told me that Vakhodia planned to kill Kallinova, and you and me."

She stared at me. "So the colonists survived?"

"The Pharan said they'd led them to safety."

"They didn't say where?"

"To their nests in the jungle?" I suggested.

She gripped my arm. "If they communicated with the colonists, Jon, then their secret is out. Did they say *how* they'd communicated?"

"They just said they led the colonists to safety."

We sat in silence for a time, staring at each other.

I said, "So, what do we do?"

Octavia looked back to where Vakhodia and Šarović were sleeping. "Hell, I don't know how to disable their lasers, even if I had the opportunity. And with Stent over there…"

"I don't feel like sleeping with them standing over us."

"So we don't," she said. "We don't even feign sleep. When it's their turn to take a watch, we'll remain awake, say we saw movement in the jungle and that it'd be suicide to sleep now."

"Right. And then?"

She thought about it, chewing her lip. "You said Vakhodia won't try to get rid of us until he gets what he wants? So we're safe until we reach the ship, at least."

"Vakhodia's been fine with me giving the orders so far," I said. "So on the last leg of the journey, we fall back and let Šarović or Stent lead the way. When we reach the ship, we disappear."

"And attempt to find the colonists?" she asked.

"That would make sense, yes."

We moved back to where Vakhodia and Šarović were sleeping, then turned our attention to the jungle.

Vakhodia slept beyond the time his watch should have started, but Šarović – like the soldier he was – woke on time.

He was about to wake his boss, but I said, "Leave him. He'd be little use, anyway. Let him sleep."

I had no desire to have any more dealings with Vakhodia than absolutely necessary; part of me wondered if, when he awoke, I'd be able to keep my feelings from him.

Indicating the jungle, Octavia said to Šarović, "We'll keep watch with you. There's been movement in there."

"Join Stent at that end," I said. "We'll stay here."

He grunted something and moved off, and I wondered how much Vakhodia had involved the mercenary in his plans. Would it be Šarović who, when the time came, put us to death?

Dawn was still another eight hours away when we set off, having breakfasted on water and dry rations. The night sky was like a bloodshot eye above the jungle when we left the outcropping and trekked higher into the foothills.

Eleven

At my suggestion, Šarović led the way. Octavia and I fell back, covering the party as we emerged from the jungle and followed a steep valley towards a rearing mountain peak.

We slogged through terrain thick with a knee-high purple grass, its serrated stems as sharp as blades. Ground-dwelling rodents teemed here, hideously ugly creatures with barbed teeth and tiny eyes. I was sure that, if they chose to attack, their teeth would be lethal. We were fortunate in that they saw us as a danger and slithered away from us in their hundreds.

I called a halt after an hour and we took a water break. I stayed away from Vakhodia and avoided eye contact.

According to the overlay map, we were a little over a kilometre from the valley where the *Persephone* had come down.

Šarović was eager to lead the way, either his military training or something competitive in his nature driving him to be the first to set eyes on the wreckage of the starship. I was more than happy to give rein to his ego. Stent followed him, then Vakhodia. Octavia and I brought up the rear.

It was the longest twenty minutes of my life.

I started thinking about when we reached the ship, and wondering what Vakhodia might do then. I reasoned that he'd keep us alive until we'd located the colonists; there would be time, when we reached the *Persephone*, for Octavia and I to confer and decide how best to make our escape.

As we walked, I considered the hapless survivors of the starship's crash-landing.

They had set off two centuries ago as intrepid explorers pushing at the boundaries of human endeavour, carrying with them the combined expertise of twenty-second century humankind. I wondered if they had expected to make landfall on some Eden-like world, not this hellish jungle planet with its inimical alternation between intolerable summers and long, ice-age winters.

If that shock had not been sufficient to undermine the confidence of the strongest colonist, how might they react when we eventually reached them? They had assumed they were at the forefront of the human expansion across the unexplored wastes of space. Now they would learn that they had been overtaken, that humankind had spread amongst the stars, colonised five hundred worlds, and discovered a hundred sentient extraterrestrial species. Moreover, whatever their scientific and technological specialisms, they would now find that their expertise had been superseded, that they were, in effect, backward relics mired in a wondrous modern age.

And for one woman there would be the extra shock of finding that, for whatever reasons, someone was intent on ending her life.

But not, I thought, if I could help it.

We had been climbing a ravine for ten gruelling minutes when, from up ahead, Šarović called out, "There it is!"

He had paused on the crest of the rise and struck a pose with one hand on his hip, the other pointing ahead through the bloody twilight.

Vakhodia joined him, clapping a hand on the mercenary's shoulder.

We caught up with the pair and I stared down at the broken-backed starship that lay in the valley, a tragically monumental sight that stirred something deep within me.

The earlier view of the ship from the drone had failed to communicate the fact of its vast dimensions. Half a kilometre long, it slumped in the cradle of rock like some defeated beast, its curving upper superstructure encumbered with a mat of vegetation; here and there, great square panels were missing and showed as black patches in the greenery. Down one side of the ship's starboard flank was a rent like a lightning flash.

I stared around for any sign of human activity, or evidence of human existence, but saw nothing.

Šarović led the way down into the valley and, slowly, we approached the starship. Octavia and I allowed the others to get well ahead of us and, as they neared the vast engine assembly at the rear of the ship, they were reduced to the size of ants in relation to the stranded behemoth.

They made their way along the flank of the *Persephone*, and I made to follow them.

Octavia stopped me with a hand on my arm. "I was right," she said, pointing to an expanse of sloping rock beside the ship. It rose towards the foothills that folded away to the distant mountain peak.

"I'm sure Vakhodia could have brought the smallship down here," she went on, "but he feared being detected by the surveillance satellites."

I scanned ahead for cover. "So when do we make ourselves scarce?"

She stared at the ship, frowning. "There's little cover in the foothills. But maybe there'll be places we can conceal ourselves within the ship."

I gripped my handgun, its butt slippery in my sweating palm.

Vakhodia and Šarović moved towards the rent in the ship's side, while Stent stationed himself a hundred metres away. He squatted on his massive haunches on the sloping grey rock, keeping watch.

Vakhodia and Šarović passed into the ship, clambering over rocks to do so, and a minute later we heard the tycoon's voice echoing in the vessel's vaulting central chamber. "Hello!"

I exchanged a glance with Octavia. She nodded, and we followed them inside.

It was like entering a cathedral that had been gutted by fire, desecrated, and reduced to a plaything of nature. The bulkheads between the sections had collapsed on impact, creating one vast empty cavern cross-hatched by broken galleries and walkways. In the distance was the triangular portal to the first coldsleep chamber. I imagined the horror of the survivors when they had been resuscitated to find that over a thousand of their compatriots had perished in the crash-landing.

Vakhodia and Šarović moved aft, picking their way through a tangle of undergrowth towards where the crew quarters had been situated.

From time to time, Šarović called out a futile greeting, "Hello there..."

Silently, Octavia touched my arm and gestured in the opposite direction. I followed her gaze. A hundred metres away, towards the coldsleep chambers, a cross gantry and several walkways had come down to form a mass of twisted metal which the native vegetation had covered in its inexorable invasion. It would make the perfect place to conceal ourselves.

Vakhodia and Šarović passed out of sight towards the crew quarters, and I followed Octavia as she crept towards the tangle of fallen walkways.

We slipped through a shroud of hanging vines, pushing our way into a scented mass of blooms. Octavia found a flight of steps, masked by foliage, and climbed. I followed until we were perhaps twenty metres above the deck, then crouched beside her as she carefully parted a curtain of vines and peered down.

The pair did not show themselves for some time, and then Vakhodia appeared, followed by the mercenary. They looked around the vast space, two diminutive figures dwarfed by the gargantuan architecture; Vakhodia said something to Šarović.

I was aware of my heartbeat, and assured myself that there was no way that they might locate us.

They stepped into the centre of the chamber, turning to take in its entirety, then Vakhodia signalled to the mercenary, who called out, "James! Carrera!"

Silence followed, broken only by the churring of some distant insect-analogue.

I saw them tense and level their weapons. Directly below us, I heard a commotion in the vegetation, and a second later something burst from the cover. I felt a surge of retrospective dread at the thought that we must have passed just metres from the creature – something that resembled a wild boar, but with too many legs. It charged towards the men, and for a second I wondered if Vakhodia's mission would end in ignominious death.

Then Šarović raised his laser in expert fashion and shot the creature dead.

It dropped, its momentum carrying it towards the mercenary who stepped nimbly out of the way. The pair regarded the creature, then Vakhodia muttered something to his henchman.

I wondered if he assumed we'd fallen foul of the monstrosity.

Vakhodia turned in a full circle, and this time it was he who called out, "James! Carrera!"

They waited in silence, staring at each other, then Vakhodia lifted his gaze and stared up at the vegetation that festooned the ship's criss-crossing walkways. His gaze passed over where we crouched. He turned and said something to Šarović, and for a second I feared he'd spotted us and was ordering the mercenary to ascend the walkways in pursuit.

If he had done so, the order was never obeyed. Seconds later the Voronian bellowed something from outside the ship. It was the first time I had heard the alien utter a sound, and his voice was in keeping with his appearance, low and rumbling.

"*Va-kho-dia!*"

Down below, the two men hurried towards the rent in the side of the ship and disappeared from sight.

Octavia touched my arm, indicating a gantry that sloped towards the jagged tear in the hull of the ship. Crouching, she stepped from the staircase onto the gantry. I followed, creeping along behind her and keeping a keen eye on the deck far below.

Octavia stopped, knelt and nodded towards the gap. From this elevation, we had a clear view of the gently shelving rock where Stent had crouched.

He was on his feet now. He'd spotted something and was pointing up the slope.

"There…" Octavia whispered.

At first I was unable to make out what she'd seen – then my vision adjusted to the distance, and to the crinkling heat haze that rose from the rock, and I saw what appeared to be a length of metal.

"And there, ten metres further up the incline." She laughed and went on, "Good God, look! All the way up – there's dozen of them, Jon! They can only be markers of some kind."

I saw the first one, and the second, then many more as I looked up. She was right. The strategically placed debris marked a route through the foothills, zigzagging its way towards a high shelf and what appeared to be the mouth of a distant cave.

"The Pharan," I said. "The Pharan led the colonists to safety, underground – and perhaps the survivors returned to scavenge the wreckage, and marked the way back to the cave for future reference."

I hesitated, then said, "But if the colonists are there, in the cave, then Vakhodia –"

Octavia shook her head. "They'll be underground, Jon. Far underground, where the Pharan dwell in summer and winter, right? The Pharan wouldn't have left them in a cave near the surface."

Vakhodia had realised the significance of the trail, and was pointing up the incline as he spoke to Šarović. Then he turned and stared down at the ship. I wondered if he was considering the wisdom of continuing without us.

As we watched, he pulled something from inside his coolsuit and unrolled it – his softscreen.

He tapped the screen, then raised it to his mouth and spoke.

"The drone," Octavia said. "He's giving commands to the drone, Jon."

Even as she said this, something flew into sight above the trio – presumably the same one that had surveyed the *Persephone* earlier – then swooped towards the ship. It paused, hovering, just outside the rent, and remained there. I imagined its probing eye fixed on the entrance, ready to report our emergence to its master.

Vakhodia and Šarović turned and began climbing, the Voronian bringing up the rear as they followed the zigzag trail of metal struts and spars up the incline. As we watched, the trio passed in and out of sight as their ascent took them into cuttings and gulleys, working their way ever further into the foothills towards the distant entrance of the cave.

I indicated the hovering drone. "The bastard's taking no chances."

"What do you reckon?"

I cursed. "We need to follow them," I said. "You know what he wants to do when he finds the colonists. And..." I went on, struck by a sudden terrible thought.

"Jon?"

"For whatever reason, he's intent on killing this woman, Kallinova, right?"

"Go on."

"So what about the fate of all the others? Will he let them live, witnesses to the killing? I doubt it."

She stared at me.

"We can't sit tight and take the risk of him slaughtering the colonists," I said.

"So we take down the drone and follow them?"

I considered the options, and realised there were none. "We wait till they enter the cave, give it a few minutes, then laser the drone. He won't necessarily assume that we brought it down."

Octavia indicated a sloping catwalk above her. "If I get high enough, I can aim *down* at the drone – so its camera won't pick up the beam."

"Five minutes after Vakhodia enters the cave, do it."

We turned our attention to the trio and watched their slow ascent through the foothills.

Octavia was silent. I sensed, somehow, that she was considering yet another option.

She turned to me and said, quietly, "What's the range of these things, Jon?" hefting the laser rifle in her grip.

It was a thought that had occurred to me, too. "Half a kay, tops."

She frowned. "How's your aim?"

"At this distance, not that good. And if we didn't take out Vakhodia and Šarović cleanly, I wouldn't want the mercenary coming after us. And even if we did, that'd leave us with Stent to deal with."

"So what do you suggest?"

I thought about it. "We'll down the drone, then follow them into the cave. I reckon we'll have time to catch up with them before they locate the colonists."

"And then?" she asked.

"We'll cross that bridge –" I began.

Octavia nudged me and pointed through the gap.

High in the foothills, the trio was approaching the mouth of the cave. As we looked on, they passed into its shadows and disappeared from sight.

We gave it five minutes, then Octavia stood and approached the slanting walkway. She stepped onto it – testing the metal to ensure it would take her weight – and climbed carefully up the slope.

She reached its highest point, lay down like a sniper and took aim with her rifle.

She waited, breathing hard and steadying her aim.

Then she gave it the briefest pulse. The beam lanced down on the drone, striking its body. The drone exploded, its remains cartwheeling through the air and shattering on the rock far below.

Octavia returned to my side and we crouched, anxiously watching the cave mouth in case Vakhodia decided to return to investigate the sudden dysfunction of his drone.

After five minutes, Octavia nodded. "We go?"

"We go," I said, and led the way down to the deck.

We lost no time and climbed into the foothills, following the trail of debris leading to the cave mouth.

I wondered at the reaction of the colonists when Vakhodia, Šarović and Stent showed themselves. They would be incredulous, of course, at the miraculous appearance of the trio. Would they assume this was a rescue mission, that Vakhodia had somehow followed them through space and tracked them to this infernal planet where they must have assumed they'd spend the rest of their lives? And then jubilation would turn to horror when Vakhodia's true motives became apparent.

We scrambled the last few metres to the mouth of the cave, hauled ourselves onto the ledge and paused for breath. I peered inside: a wide, low opening receding into darkness.

We activated our shoulder-lamps, levelled our lasers, and entered the cave.

The walls on either side drew back to form an oval chamber perhaps five metres across. In the distance where the cavern narrowed I made out a high, thin aperture in the grey stone, just wide enough to admit the Voronian's bulk. Octavia led the way and passed through the gap. My lamp illuminated her jungle-green armour, moving cautiously a few metres ahead.

The ground sloped. We were passing down a narrow corridor, perhaps two metres wide, a natural fissure in the rock. I feared that the way might narrow even further, so that Stent had been unable to continue and we might run into him.

My fear was ill-founded – the reverse was true: the corridor widened and the walls exhibited evidence of having being chiselled. Octavia stopped, silently indicating a line of bas relief figures carved into the grey rock: a hundred tiny representations of the Pharan, receding into the distance. As we hurried on, I felt a wave of awe as I considered the age of the carvings. The Pharan had achieved sentience half a million years ago, by human reckoning. These carvings might have been in existence well before *Homo sapiens* came down from the trees.

The corridor fell away steeply before us, and it was all we could do not to go slipping and slithering down the incline as we hurried on our way. The tiny carved figures ceased, to be replaced by cruder representations of native wildlife. Ahead, Octavia slowed and raised a warning hand. I crept along behind her, my heartbeat loud in my ears.

She turned to me and killed her shoulder-lamp, gesturing for me to do the same. In the darkness, she moved her head closer and whispered, almost below her breath, "Hear that?"

A distant, thrumming sound, familiar yet hard to place.

"A generator?" she murmured.

I gripped my laser.

"And look," she said.

Now that my eyes had become accustomed to the darkness, I made out, far ahead, a dim glow illuminating the arch of the corridor.

I felt her breath against my cheek as she whispered, "Follow me. If Vakhodia and Šarović start shooting the colonists, I go for Vakhodia, you Šarović, okay?"

"Okay. And Stent?"

"Whoever's closest," she said without missing a beat.

She turned and crept forward, and I followed.

Ahead, the dim glow brightened as we approached its source. The thrumming of the generator increased. I felt my stomach turn at the inevitability of the imminent confrontation.

The corridor widened, opened out as it approached a high, cavernous chamber. Octavia was a black outline against the faint light, moving as lithe as a panther towards a spur of rock that overlooked the body of the cavern. She ducked behind it. Taking a breath, I hurried after her.

She pointed down into the natural amphitheatre of the subterranean chamber, and I followed the direction of her outstretched finger.

At the far end of the cavern I made out a stack of machinery and parts salvaged from the *Persephone*, a line of what looked like bunks standing against the curving wall, a machine workshop and a communal eating area made up of tables and chairs fashioned out of debris salvaged from the ship. The makeshift encampment was illuminated by a dozen flickering arc-lamps.

If the camp was bedraggled and careworn, then its inhabitants were even more so. Perhaps a hundred men and women stood in a semi-circle in the middle of the cavern, staring ahead in silence. They were thin and malnourished and dressed in rags, the men with beards and long, ragged hair. Although every man and woman down there would be no more than thirty, an unwitting observer would have put then at twenty or thirty years older.

I wondered if these were the only survivors, or if others dwelled in deeper caverns.

Vakhodia, Šarović and Stent must have emerged from the shadows only minutes earlier, for there were still some straggling colonists making their way from the rear of the cavern to join their staring compatriots.

We looked on, tense, as Vakhodia and Šarović stepped forward, fifty metres from us, and faced the colonists – with Stent standing silently off to one side.

I was too far away to make out the expressions on the faces of the colonists as they regarded the human pair – evidence that something momentous had occurred during the two hundred years they had been in coldsleep. Their collective demeanour was that of a Greek chorus reduced to silence by the enormity of what they were apprehending.

Then Vakhodia stepped forward and called out, "Anna Kallinova?" It was at once a question and a command.

Beside me, Octavia tensed.

The colonists parted, shuffling aside as a tall figure moved from their midst and stood before Vakhodia. She might have been elegant, once, even regal, but now she was a pathetic figure reduced to skin and bone. Even so, she drew herself upright, tragically proud, as she faced the tycoon.

They spoke, but we were too far away for me to make out what was said.

I leaned towards Octavia and murmured, "How's your aim at fifty metres?"

"Not good – and Vakhodia and Šarović are standing right in front of the colonists. I couldn't be sure of hitting either of them without risking the others."

"So what do you suggest?"

"We hold fire," she counselled.

In the amphitheatre, Vakhodia raised his voice, and what he said mystified me, "You betrayed me!"

Octavia gripped my arm. "What the hell?"

The woman replied, more softly, but even so I made out, "... always were an obsessive fool..."

They exchanged more heated words, too hurried to make out, and then Vakhodia reached for the handgun at his side, drew it and directed its sleek, needle-barrel at the woman.

Beyond him, the colonists gave a collective gasp of incredulity.

Octavia raised her laser and aimed – then cursed. "If I miss Vakhodia..."

I raised my laser, too, and took aim, but lowered it in fear of hitting the colonists.

Then, without thinking about what I was doing, and before Octavia could stop me, I stood up and moved from behind the rock, and walked down the gently shelving incline towards Vakhodia, Šarović and the woman.

In retrospect, I wonder if what I did was prompted in part by guilt – guilt at my part in Solange Delacroix's death – and a subconscious desire for atonement.

At the time, though, all I thought about was preventing Vakhodia from taking the life of Anna Kallinova.

Šarović turned and brought his laser to bear on my chest. "Stop right there!" he commanded.

I halted, and his shouted order alerted Vakhodia who turned on his heel and stared at me. In the dim illumination from the arc-lights, he gave an icy smile. "Mr James, back from the dead."

He lifted his handgun and aimed.

"Think about what you're doing, Vakhodia," I said in desperation. "Don't add murder to your other crimes."

From the corner of my eye, I made out the hulking figure of Stent moving closer to me. I wondered if I would have time to raise my laser, account for Vakhodia, then swing to fire at the Voronian before he pounced.

"My other crimes? You mean trespassing on Pharantara –?"

"Lower your weapon," I coaxed. "The authorities will do no more than issue you with a fine for transgressing protected territory."

He laughed in derision. "On your knees!" he shouted. "Hands in the air!"

I obeyed. I glanced behind Vakhodia at the woman – her drawn face a mask of fear – and at the other colonists, more than ever now a Greek chorus reduced to the role of impotent spectators.

"I will take great pleasure in executing you, James."

Gripping the handgun in his trembling left hand, Vakhodia took aim at my head. From the corner of my eye, I saw the Voronian approaching.

I lifted my laser – but before I could fire, Stent moved.

In my long if infrequent association with members of extraterrestrial races, I've often had occasion to wonder at the values we shared. I am certain that Stent – despite his bovine, lumpen aspect – was motivated at that moment by a sense of honour, loyalty, and *quid pro quo*.

I stared across at Vakhodia, and I swear I saw his finger move towards the firing stud.

Then Stent reached the tycoon and knocked the handgun from his grip, reached out and grabbed him by the neck. He raised his outstretched arm with seemingly no effort at all, lifting Vakhodia from his feet.

To my right, Šarović loosed off a laser beam at the Voronian, but it merely ricochetted off his impervious hide.

As I watched, Stent squeezed his massive fingers and Vakhodia screamed, then gagged, as his face turned purple and his eyes popped. Šarović fired again, to no avail. The Voronian increased his pressure, squeezing his massive fingers, and blood oozed down his raised arm as Vakhodia died, his feet kicking pathetically as he did so.

Šarović fired again and again, the electric blue laser beam bouncing off the Voronian and erratically illuminating the cavern. Then the mercenary turned and aimed at where I still knelt – and Octavia stepped from behind the spur of rock and killed Šarović with a single laser beam to the head.

Stent gave a moan – at the belated realisation of what he had done? – then dropped the lifeless, rag-doll form of Vakhodia to the ground, turned and barrelled past me.

I staggered to my feet and gave chase, propelled by the sudden desire to comfort, and thank, my alien saviour.

Stent charged from the cavern, moving with deceptive speed for a creature of such bulk. I followed, entering the tunnel and staring ahead to where my dancing shoulder-lamp illuminated the Voronian's retreating form.

He pulled away from me, driven by who knows what complex alien guilt, and I slackened my pace, exhausted. I called his name from time to time, but guessed that my efforts would be futile.

I hurried towards the surface, leaving behind the subterranean chill and moving towards the heat of the Pharantaran night. By the time I came to the mouth of the cave, I was exhausted.

I stood on the high ledge, breathing hard, and stared down across the rumpled foothills.

There was no sign of the Voronian.

I sat down, my back against the rock, and heard movement to my right. Octavia emerged from the cave and joined me on the ledge.

"The Pharan will find him," she said, quietly. "They'll take care of him, Jon."

She sat down beside me and we stared out across the alien jungle that extended without interruption to the far, curving horizon of the planet.

Twelve

I had intended to go back down to the cavern and speak with the colonists; there was a lot to explain, after all. In the event, a colonist came to us, and it was she who offered an explanation.

Anna Kallinova stepped hesitantly from the mouth of the cave, smiled unsurely at me, and drawing her ragged blouse across her chest, sat down before us.

She was silent for a time, then said in a voice so soft I had to lean forward to make out her words, "I think I owe you an explanation."

I said, "Vakhodia... He was from your time, right?"

She stared down at her upturned hands in the bowl of her lap. "We were lovers, two hundred years ago. I met Santor Vakhodia at university, where we were studying cryogenics. We were both dreamers – envisaging humankind's push out to the stars in great slowships." She shook her head. "We shared a vision, and I suppose it was inevitable that we became lovers. Santor graduated and formed his own company. He was brilliant, and employed the finest minds to develop coldsleep technology. I worked as an engineer for his company, and for a while... for a while things were truly wonderful between us. And then," – she shrugged – "something in his nature, his obsession, the coldness at the core of his being... Well, it drove me away, killed whatever love I'd felt for him. I left Santor and eventually met someone else." She fell silent, staring out across the alien world. "To say that Santor took it badly would be an understatement. He attacked the man I loved, badly injuring him – only Santor's wealth and eminence in the scientific community saved him from being jailed. Then he targeted me, and for five years made my life a misery, trailing me with avatars of himself describing in horrible, graphic detail what he intended to do to me. He always was controlling, of his business interests, of people. It was all about *power*. During that time, his company went from strength to strength, made significant breakthroughs in cryogenic science, and won the contract to equip the first slowships with coldsleep technology. He invested his profits in founding an asteroid mining company, and never lost an opportunity to inform me of his wealth. As if I was ever concerned about things like that." She shrugged, smiling from me to Octavia, then went on, "My husband and I – he was also an engineer – signed up as colonists aboard the *Persephone*, and we were accepted. The irony that I was fleeing Earth, as well as Santor Vakhodia, aboard a vessel enabled by his technology, was not lost on me."

"The coldsleep tech," I said. "He utilised the technology he'd developed to sleep away the centuries. To gain his revenge…"

She shook her head, surprising me. "No," she said. "I mean, I don't think that was his initial motivation – to come after me. When we were together, in the early days of coldsleep development, he often spoke about how he would use it. It was always his intention to use coldsleep to travel into the future, waking from time to time to monitor his investments, guide the direction of his business interests. He wanted to be in control of his empire for ever. I think it must have been incidental that he heard about the *Persephone* and formulated his plan to come after me. Imagine my shock an hour ago when he suddenly appeared. It was unbelievable, a nightmare."

"He hired me to guide him here," I said. "I had no idea, at the start, what he was planning –"

She murmured, "I often wondered, back then, how his love could have turned to so much hate." She smiled, sadly. "How could I have guessed that it would end here, light years away from Earth where it all began?"

We were silent for a time, lost in our own thoughts.

At last I said, "Now, I think I owe you an explanation."

She smiled, reached out and touched my arm with a hand that was all skin and bone. "We worked it out, in the long hours we had to think things through over the course of the past two years."

Octavia leaned forward. "Worked it out?"

"That humankind had already spread among the stars."

Octavia shook her head. "But how?"

"When we phased-in here and came down in the valley," Anna said, "and were resuscitated from coldsleep to discover what had happened... We lost over two thousand men and women in the crash," she said. "Fewer than a thousand of us survived, and over the years... Well, what with disease, and starvation – only two hundred of us remain. But," she went on brightly, smiling at us through her despair, "we owe our survival to the Pharan."

"The Pharan?" I said, my stomach turning. "They... they *communicated* with you?"

I exchanged a worried glance with Octavia.

Anna shook her head in wonder. "That was the astounding thing," she murmured. "Imagine our astonishment when the Pharan emerged from the jungle, approached us – and spoke our language! Imagine that!"

Fearfully, I said, "They *spoke* to you?"

She nodded. "Spoke, in a fair approximation of our language. At first we thought they must be telepathic" – she laughed at this – "but then they explained."

Octavia leaned forward. "Explained?" she said.

"They told us that a ship had landed on Pharantara before us," Anna said, "and they had communicated with people who called themselves human. They said that they had learned our language, and that one member of the human team had acted in a way that had earned him the ever-lasting gratitude of the Pharan."

I swallowed, unable to bring myself to speak.

"He saved the life of one of their kind," she said.

97

Octavia looked across at me, smiling with tenderness.

Anna went on, "So we knew that humankind had pushed out from Earth while we journeyed through sub-space, our technology superseded by a kind greater, faster. Our dismay was tempered by the hope that, one day, we might be rescued."

She fell silent and stared out over the jungle.

"Soon," Octavia said, "a USO ship will arrive, and take you away."

Anna smiled, wide-eyed, and whispered, "To experience the future..."

Later, after she had left us to rejoin her husband and the other colonists, I ordered my imp to summon the smallship.

We sat on the ledge high in the foothills, looking out over the jungle in silence, and awaited its arrival.

A little later, Octavia reached into her coolsuit and pulled something out – a silver ziplock bag.

I watched her as she opened the bag and stared at the silvery-blue powder glinting within.

"Matha?" I said.

"Back at the place where the khata captured Stent, when I said I'd tripped." She shrugged. "I saw a matha plant and grabbed the stamen. And look, it's crystallised already."

I stared at the scintillating powder. "Enough for what? Another three years, four?"

She pursed her lips, staring at the drug. "Five, I'd say. Maybe more."

She was silent for a while, before saying in a whisper, "This stuff reminds me of Garcia."

I looked at her. "How's that?"

"Gives me a good time for a while," she replied, smiling, "then runs out on me."

Surprising me, she stood quickly and strode to the edge of the ledge. She tipped the bag. The powder cascaded out, glittering like diamond filings as it caught the light of the sun.

She looked at me. "This trip was about more than me getting a high," she said.

She sat down and leaned back against the cool rock, and I looped an arm around her shoulders and drew her towards me.

Octavia and I spent the following night aboard the smallship.

I slept badly, plagued by dreams – I was in the jungle again, and Solange was calling my name, begging me to save her.

I came awake in the early hours, dressed and made my way through the ship. I was not sure whether I was calling to the Pharan, or if they were calling me. At any rate, I had something important to tell them, and as it turned out they had something to impart to me, too.

I activated the sliding door and stood at the top of the ramp as the door sighed shut behind me. I felt as if the ghost of Solange was by my side.

I looked down the incline to the shadowy silent bulk of the *Persephone*, semi-shrouded in alien vegetation. Above it, a scatter of stars scintillated. The night was hot; my coolsuit kicked in and I took a deep breath of the balmy air.

Then I saw the alien.

He was seated cross-legged at the foot of the ramp, as if awaiting me.

As soon as I noticed him, he stood and made the hands-to-chest beckoning gesture of his kind.

"I must tell you something," I began, following him away from the smallship and down the incline.

He had skipped away, a shadow in the night, but I could sense the presence of his mind, and a mass of others a little way beyond.

They were seated in a semi-circle on the bare rock before the *Persephone*, perhaps a hundred of them, watching me as I approached and sat down.

I felt the balm of their massed minds ease my fears.

"I must tell you," I said, "that soon a ship from Earth will land on Pharantara, and many humans will come here to take away the colonists. You must go from here, have no contact with the humans."

Even as I spoke, I could feel their compliance washing over me, reassuring me.

"We will soon be gone," they replied, *"to our underground abode for the duration of summer. There will be no more contact between our kind and yours. This, now, between us... this will be the last."*

I nodded, smiling my relief.

They spoke again. *"We feel your pain, Jonathan."*

"My pain?"

"We share what you feel. We understand."

I stared at the silent aliens ranged in a wide arc, squatting in the lee of the starship, watching me with their massive eyes, and I felt a sudden unstoppable surge of gratitude and affection at their expression of empathy.

They said, *"We wish to thank you, Jonathan, for what you did many sunrises ago."*

"You thanked me," I said, "at the time."

"We did not fully understand your pain, then," they said.

"And now?"

"Now we have come to understand what you feel, your guilt, and we have agreed on how to help you."

I smiled and shook my head, and knew that they were mistaken in assuming that they could assuage my grief, or my guilt.

They said, "We will give you *our* collective memory of that day, Jonathan."

"No!" I cried. "No, not that..."

My own memories were more than enough – more than I could bear at times – and I did not want the added pain of reliving the incident from their alien perspective.

But in their collective wisdom, they overrode my desire.

I was flooded with a sudden wave of images, emotions, and I was back in the jungle again, on that fateful day three years ago.

Solange and I were collecting botanical samples, or rather she was doing the collecting and I was standing guard. We had made love that morning, and the recollection of our intimacy was still a warm glow within me as I watched her bend, scoop, fill the sample containers, rise and smile at me, move on and exclaim in delight at discovering a new plant.

Later we were joined by a small alien – a child – who had taken to following us on our forays into the jungle.

We had moved further from the ship, on the trail of the spore of an iris-analogue, watched by the curious alien child, when she cried out in alarm, but too late.

Something whipped with lightning speed from the undergrowth to our right – and whipped again – and suddenly, within the space of a second, I was alone.

I cried out, raised my laser, gave chase. And stopped, staring, at what confronted me.

Two great bloated putrescent plants, each twice as tall as a man, stood in a clearing in the jungle, and Solange and the small Pharan were lashed to their boles by suckered tendrils. Solange stared at me in wide-eyed terror and screamed her pain.

And the small alien reached out with her mind and showed me what to do.

I had no choice. I acted on impulse, I later told myself. The plant that had captured the alien child was closer to me, after all.

I lifted my laser, aimed at where the tendril connected with the tree branch high above, and I fired. The bloated bole that had captured the alien child seemed to deflate, its tendrils relax, and the Pharan fell insensate from its grasp.

And instantly I swung the laser and fired a long beam at the goitrous junction of tendril and branch above the plant which had captured Solange.

The tendrils relaxed their grip, released her, and she slumped face forward to the jungle floor.

I recalled only fragments of what happened next. My incredulous realisation that my lover was dead... My cries of pain... Holding her body, rocking her back and forth in my inconsolable grief... The realisation that if I had attempted to save Solange first, then she might have lived...

Then the arrival of a hundred chattering Pharan, soon silenced as they beheld me, and took up the child and gave joyous thanks that she was alive.

I had picked up Solange, and carried her back to the smallship, and an hour later we had lifted-off from Pharantara.

And now, as I sat before the Pharan in the balmy scented night, my head hanging as I sobbed, they filled my senses with a new emotion: the recollected surge of the mother's elation that her daughter was alive – a joy amplified as it was transmitted to a hundred, a thousand, ten thousand, receptive minds across the jungle. A joy that grew, transmuted by the realisation not only of how the girl had been saved, but by whom.

Now the Pharans' remembered joy at the child's salvation became a tidal wave directed at my puny human mind, an overwhelming ocean of emotion that lifted me, buoyed me with a sensation I had never before experienced. The heartfelt gratitude of an entire race in response to my actions hit me in a rush, making me gasp aloud and weep with joy – and then, slowly, it receded to leave a residue, a warm glow at the core of my being that I knew would never leave me, would never diminish.

I came to my senses, returned to the present, and looked up to find the Pharan regarding me in silence.

Their facial expressions were unreadable, but in their minds I sensed satisfaction at the gift they had bequeathed me – an ineradicable joy to counterpoint my grief.

I rose slowly to my feet and lifted a heavy hand at the thought of our parting.

"*Farewell, Jonathan,*" they said as one.

"Goodbye," I replied.

The aliens stood as one and slipped away into the shadows, and I turned and made my way back to the smallship.

At the foot of the ramp, I paused. "Imp," I said, "play the audio cache from Lysenko back in '71."

Are you sure, Jonathan? it asked.

"I'm sure," I said. "Play it."

And as Solange Delacroix's voice sounded softly in my head, I climbed the ramp and turned.

I stood there for a long time, staring out across the jungle, as Arcturus rose on another new day.

About the Author

Born in Haworth, West Yorkshire, Eric Brown has lived in Australia, India and Greece. He has won the British Science Fiction Award twice for his short stories, and his novel *Helix Wars* was shortlisted for the 2012 Philip K. Dick award. He's published over seventy books and his latest novel is the eighth in the Langham and Dupré mystery series, set in the 1950s, *Murder at Standing Stone Manor*. He lives near Dunbar in Scotland, and his website is at: <u>ericbrown.co.uk</u>

NP Novellas

1: Universal Language – Tim Major

A murder mystery that pays homage to Asimov's seminal robot stories and also to classic detective tales. A scientist has been murdered in an airlock-sealed lab on Mars, and the only possible culprit is a robot incapable of harming humans...

2: Worldshifter – Paul Di Filippo

High-octane SF reminiscent of Jack Vance but wholly Di Filippo in its execution. Klom is forced into a desperate chase across the stars, pursued by the most powerful beings in the galaxy, after he stumbles on a secret in the bowels of an antique ship.

3: May Day – Emma Coleman

Orphaned during wartime at just seventeen, May continues with the silly superstitions her mum taught her. Until the one time she doesn't; at which point something dark and deadly arises, and proceeds to invade her life, determined to claim her as its own...

4: Requiem for an Astronaut – Daniel Bennett

30 years ago, astronaut Joan Kaminsky disappeared while testing an experimental craft powered by alien technology. Now, her glowing figure starts to appear in the sky, becoming a focus for anti-tech cults. One man, who knew Joan, determines to find out why.

5: Rose Knot – Kari Sperring

Kari Sperring, historian and award-winning fantasy author, delivers a gripping tale of love, infidelity, loyalty, misguided intentions and the price of nobility, featuring some lesser known members of Arthur's court: the sons of Lot, the Orkney royal family.

Also From Newcon Press

Blackthorn Winter – Liz Williams

Something is coming for the Fallow sisters, for their friends and their lovers, but they have no idea what, and their mother Alys is no help as she's gone wandering again, though she did promise to return by Christmas, and December is already here... In this sequel to *Comet Weather*, four fey sisters are drawn ever further from the familiar world of contemporary London and their Somerset home into darker realms where no one is who they seem and nothing is to be trusted...

Edge of Heaven – RB Kelly

In the honeycomb districts of the Creo Basse, Boston Turrow is searching desperately for meds for his epileptic sister when he encounters one of the many ways Creo can kill a person. His rescuer is Danae Grant, a woman recently made homeless. Danae knows people, Boston knows where she can stay... When a deadly plague erupts among the populace, the pair determine to discover the dark secret behind the outbreak.

London Centric – Edited by Ian Whates

Future Tales of London. Neal Asher, Mike Carey, Geoff Ryman, Aliette de Bodard, Dave Hutchinson, Aliya Whiteley, Eugen Bacon and more. Militant A.I.s, virtual realities, augmented realities and alternative realities; a city where murderers stalk the streets, where drug lords rule from the shadows, and where large sections of the population are locked in time stasis, but where tea is still sipped in cafés on the corner and the past still resonates with the future...

Shadows on the Hillside – Ed by Storm Constantine

An anthology of stories that take the reader deep into the strangeness of landscape, where reality flickers like summer's heat, weirdness generates inexplicable events that mystify and intrigue – asking questions that can never fully be answered. Stories yet untold: a secret in the earth, a cry that shakes the air yet cannot be heard by the human ear. Something happened in these places, but what...? *Shadows on the Hillside* is one of the final literary projects by the irreplaceable Storm Constantine.

www.newconpress.co.uk

Lightning Source UK Ltd.
Milton Keynes UK
UKHW041128201121
394223UK00003B/109